Ain't No Savage Like the One I Got 2

Tina J.

Ain't No Savage Like the One I Got 2

Copyright © 2016 by Tina J.

More books from me:

The Thug I Chose 1, 2 & 3

A Thin Line Between Me and My Thug 1 & 2

I Got Luv For My Shawty 1 & 2

Kharis and Caleb: A Different Kind of Love 1 & 2

Loving You Is A Battle 1 & 2 & 3

Violet and The Connect 1 & 2 & 3

You Complete Me

Love Will Lead You Back

This Thing Called Love

Are We In This Together 1 & 2

Shawty Down To Ride For a Boss 1 & 2

When A Boss Falls in Love 1, 2 & 3

Let Me Be The One

We Got That Forever Love

Ain't No Savage Like The One I Got

Table of Contents

Previously

Colby

"Wake y'all asses up. Got some nigga downstairs banging on my door looking for you at eight in the damn morning." She looked at me and I shrugged my shoulders. "I'm not talking about him girl. I'm talking about your ass."

It was time for her to shrug my shoulders. She stood up and went to the bathroom to brush her teeth and wash her face. I followed behind her and grabbed my toothbrush, then did the same.

"Put some clothes on." I said with a mouth full of toothpaste.

"I have clothes on."

"Don't play with me." I said, and she looked down. She had on some boy shorts and a white wife beater. She put some leggings and a t-shirt on before she headed downstairs. I got closer to the living room and noticed it was some guy she called Maurice.

"Hey sexy. Long time no see." He said reaching for a hug but she pushed him back.

"What do you want Maurice?"

"I came to tell you that I miss you, and I want you back."

"Too bad, nigga; she's taken. Get your goofy ass the fuck up out of here."

"Who is this, Journey, and why is he coming from upstairs?"

"You're a dumb motherfucker. If I said she's taken, it's obvious I'm her man. I'm coming from her room, because that's what we do."

"I know you didn't give this thug your virginity and not me."

Phew! Phew!

I shot his ass in the head twice. Who the fuck did he think he was questioning my woman? He should've left when he had the chance. I sent a text to Wesley and told him to send someone over to clean up the mess I made.

"Umm, ummm, ummm. Girl, you got this nigga killing over you. You better not ever leave his crazy ass. I may not find you." Her grandmother said laughing and walking away. She didn't even care that a man was dead in the house.

"Colby, I know I never told you about my parents, but if I plan on being with you, I'm going to tell you, and I don't want you to do that in front of me again." I nodded my head, then we sat in the kitchen while she made us something to eat.

"One night, my mom could be heard downstairs begging my dad to pay someone money. My father paid the money, but whoever the guy was tacked on four thousand dollars for interest."

"Damn, that's a lot."

"That's the same thing my dad said. He didn't pay it and said he wasn't. That night, he called my brother, Haven, in the room and gave him money to buy us cell phones, summer clothes, and told him to put the rest away. Two weeks went by, and it seemed like everything was fine.

The night my parents were killed was like any other night. We had just finished eating dinner and had taken our showers and were getting ready for bed. We heard yelling downstairs, so Haven told us to come in his room. There was a secret door in his closet that had just enough room to fit the three of us in it just in case something happened. Haven made me and my brother get in and went back out to see what was going on, but he didn't know I came out to look also. I watched as this man came in and took both of my parents' life like they were nothing. Neither of them begged for their lives, and after he killed them, he stepped on my father's back like he was a piece of the floor.

I ran back into the closet, and a few minutes later, Haven was coming in behind me. We heard the men yelling out for us but none of us moved. We just stayed quiet, then fell asleep in there. When we came out the next morning, our house was trashed, and my parents' bodies were gone. It was two days later when the cops found them miles away from here and had broadcasted it on the news. That's when we were able to identify them." I saw her crying and the eggs burning, so I ran up behind her, cut the stove off, and hugged her. Now, I see why she said that when I pulled a gun out on her. I see why

3

she didn't like violence. To see your own parents murdered in cold blood was nothing I would wish on anyone.

"Did they catch the guys who did it?"

"No. I'm sure he's still out there somewhere."

"Do you know his name?"

"I will never forget his name or face. It's embedded in my head forever. Colby, I'm not a killer, but if I ever saw him again, I would take his life the way he took my mom and dad's."

"What was his name?"

"Dice." It felt like the wind was knocked out of me when she said it. I let her go and fell back against the wall. There was no way this could be happening right now, but it all started coming together... the reason why I was sent to do this. I had to get out of this house.

"Colby, are you ok?" She asked, wiping her face, but I couldn't answer her. My words were caught in my throat. I know Dice is the right person she named, because no one else had that name around there. I ran up to her room, grabbed my keys, and sprinted to my car. I passed the guys cleaning the mess up and called Wesley.

"Yo, meet me at pops', NOW!" I said in the phone and hung up. I was racing down the highway trying to get there. When I arrived, he was standing outside talking to the gardener and was dressed like he came from a wedding or some shit.

4

"You motherfucker. You knew didn't you? You fucking knew." He started laughing, and I punched him in the face and kept punching him until I felt people pulling me off him.

"What's going on?" Wesley said holding me against my car.

"This motherfucker is the reason Dice is dead."

"Dice? Why are you bringing him up?"

"Don't you want to know why our brother was killed?" When I said that, Wesley let go, turned around, and gave my father the evilest look.

"Who killed him?"

"I don't know that yet. I know that he sent Dice to kill Journey's parents, and whoever killed Dice must've found out he did it and went after him. Your father sent me to Journey to find out from her who did it and then kill her. You had me do all that, and she doesn't even know."

"No, but I do, and you taking her out would've given me the satisfaction of watching that motherfucker suffer. His entire life is based around Journey, and he will go crazy if anything happened to her. You're lucky she was able to tame that beast, because he was coming for you after you pulled that gun on her." He was getting up off the ground and spitting out blood.

"Who the fuck are you talking about?"

"Don't worry. You'll know in due time. I may have missed him that night at the club, but I won't miss again."

"I thought you were worried about Venus that night. Did you set that shit up knowing she was in there?"

"I didn't know she would be there, but that was my doing, and he killed that stupid bitch and a few of my good men. It's only a matter of time before he gets what's coming to him. Matter of fact, if I were you, I would find my way back to that girl. It would be a shame if something were to happen to her because you left her unattended."

When he said that, I was a nervous fucking wreck. I jumped back in my car and flew back to her house. When I got there, the cops and ambulance were covering the driveway and putting up caution tape.

"Baby, what happened?" I asked, when I bombarded my way in the house and saw her standing there with her grandmother.

"I don't know, Colby. After you left, Grams and I were sitting in the kitchen talking when she said she saw someone in the backyard. She made me hide in her room, and when she yelled for me to come out, there were two dead bodies in the kitchen. She said they came in and she hid in the kitchen closet.

"Your grandmother has a gun?"

"Hell yea, I got a gun. It's registered too. I know who your father is, and I've never trusted him. I told my son he was a grimy motherfucker and that he was going to get him killed." Now I was confused as hell.

"Hold on." Journey said and answered her phone.

6

"Hey Passion. What? Oh my God. I'll be there in a few minutes."

"What's the matter?"

"Grams, Haven got shot and he's at the hospital."

"I'll drive you." I told her, and the three of us jumped in the car.

"Jax, where are you? Haven got shot. Ok, I'll meet you at the hospital."

"Oh my God, please let him make it. I can't take it if he dies."

"He's going to be fine Journey. Try and relax. You can't stress the baby out." I told her.

"Oh so you know?" Her grandmother said.

"Yup and I'm happy as hell."

"Are y'all back together?"

"It's up to her. I was the one who lied and cheated trying to hide something from her when I should've just been up front. I love Journey and I understand that she needs time to make her decision. But you can bet I'll be here every day until she makes one. And if she comes back with a no, I'll still be here until she changes her mind."

"Make him suffer baby."

"Of course, Grandma. You didn't raise no fool."

"That's cold Grams. I thought you loved me."

"I do. But I love Journey more, and you have to suffer enough so that it won't happen again."

"Trust me, it won't."

We pulled up to the emergency room and she ran over to some chick that I guess was his girlfriend. I saw Jax walk in with my sister and was a bit confused. I knew that she called him, but I thought it was for Venus to comfort her. Those two exchanged hugs, and I wasn't too happy about that.

"What are you doing here?" Venus asked me and pulled me to the side.

"What you mean? I brought Grams and Journey. She said her brother was shot." As I was telling her that, Wesley walked in mad as hell and came straight to Venus and I.

"Where is that motherfucker?" He yelled out which made everyone look, including Jax.

"Who?"

"The motherfucker that killed Dice."

"Dice? How do you know him?" Journey came to where we were. The three of us stood there not saying a word.

"Colby, tell me you didn't know the man that killed my parents."

Venus covered her mouth and started crying, and Wesley had a sympathetic look. I was just staring at her because I forgot to tell her when I got back to the house.

"The family of Haven Banks." The doctor came out to say something, but all of that shit was cut short when I heard a gun cock.

"If you came here to kill my brother, then I suggest you ask God to forgive you for your sins, because I'm about to blow your fucking head off."

Jax

When I got the call from Journey that my brother was shot, it was like everything in the world stopped. I jumped up and grabbed Venus and my car keys. I was hoping and praying that he wasn't dead. We got to the hospital so fast I don't even remember driving, and that couldn't be a good thing. Journey was already there with Colby, Grams, Drew a few of our other peoples, and I saw Passion with her son. I went straight to where she was to ask what happened. I knew she was the last one with him, because I sent him a text to see if he was stepping out, and he told me he was chilling and going out to eat with her. I was happy he found someone, because Wolf was wild as hell and needed that one person to calm him down.

She started telling me how they were at a park, and as they tried to leave, they were blocked in. I asked her did she see who it was, but she told me no because Wolf made her leave after he put "four people down" as she put it. I appreciated that she knew not to say killed or murdered them. I was listening to her tell me what had happened as Wolf got to the car when I saw some nigga walk in resembling my girl talking shit about my brother. I was only aware of Colby being her brother so to see him I was confused. Journey had no idea that Wolf killed Dice, so when he said someone told him Dice's killer was in the hospital, I already knew what was up. I stood up and heard Journey ask Colby how he knew the person who killed our parents. Hell, I was interested in knowing that myself.

"If you came here to kill my brother, then I suggest you ask God to forgive you for your sins, because I'm about to blow your fucking head off." I said and had my gun on the dudes' head that came in talking shit. My girl had tears coming down her face, then Colby pulled his gun out and had it pointed at me.

"What the hell is going on?" I heard my sister yell out.

"This nigga is here to kill Wolf and you already know that shit ain't happening." I said and saw Drew walking up with his gun pointed towards Colby too.

"Wesley is it?" Journey said, and he nodded his head yes.

"Why do you want to kill my brother?"

"Your brother?" Colby and the dude Wesley said at the same time.

"Yes, my brother."

"Jax, please don't kill my brothers." I heard Venus crying, then run out the hospital. I wanted to go after her but I couldn't take the chance of these niggas running up in Wolf's room.

"Journey, your brother killed Dice." Colby was very calm when he spoke with her, and I could see how much he loved her, but that didn't make me take my gun off Wesley nor did Drew pull his back.

"He did?"

"Yes."

"I'm sorry he did that, but I told you he killed both of my parents, so if you're looking for me to feel bad, I can't." She said.

"Journey, he was my brother." She gasped and covered her mouth.

"WHAT?" My grandmother yelled out.

"That motherfucker who killed my son and daughter-in-law was your brother?" No one said anything.

"Look, the doctor is here to give us an update on my man, and y'all are standing here pointing guns at each other. My son is here as well as other innocent people. If you want to kill each other, can you pick another time to do it?" Passion rolled her eyes and asked my grandmother to go with her so he would give her the information. Wesley and Colby both put their hands up and walked out backwards. Neither of them said a word, and no one lowered their guns. Once they were out of sight, I lowered mine, walked over to where the doctor was, and listened to him tell us about Wolf.

"Thank goodness he's going to be ok." Journey said after we heard the doctor say that he was hit twice, but was expected to make a full recovery. I stepped outside to call Venus, and she answered on the first ring.

"What Jax?"

"Where are you?"

"I'm with my brothers."

11

"Are you coming back? I want to see you."

"No."

"Venus, I'm sorry about the way things went down, but I need you right now, and you know I hate sleeping alone."

"Jax, you need me and my brothers need me too. I just stood in the hospital and watched you almost kill one of them. I only know bits and pieces of what's going on, and I'm sorry that my brother did that to your parents, but I can't ignore the fact that your brother killed mine either. Jax, I don't think."

"Don't you fucking say it Venus." I knew she was trying to break up with me and I couldn't have that.

"Jax, please don't make it harder than it has to be. There's a lot going on right now between our families, and I think it's best if we go our separate ways."

"Where are you? I'm coming to you."

"It's over Jax. I will always love you, but this isn't going to work. Goodbye."

I couldn't believe she was mad that I was about to kill her brother. Shit, he came in there to kill mine, but I'm supposed to be ok with that? She on some bullshit, and if that was what she was on then it was best that we did stay away from each other.

I hopped in my car to go to my house. I packed all her shit up and put it in the U-Haul that I still had until tomorrow to move her things in. I drove over to her house and left all that shit in front of her door. If she wanted to be done with me,

12

fine, but I wasn't putting shit in her house. I picked my phone up and sent her a text message.

Me: *You wanted your space so I'm giving it to you. Your stuff is back at your house, so there's no need for you to come back over.*

I hit send and waited for her to respond. I heard my phone go off and it was a message from her.

My wife: *Jax, I would've come to get it, but that's fine.*

Me: *One last thing. I will be at all your appointments, and you better let me know when you go into labor. Fuck with it if you want.*

My wife: *Ok Jax. I wouldn't do that to you. I know how much you want our child. Us not being together is not going to stop me from allowing you to be there. Goodbye.*

I put my phone down on the seat and drove back to the hospital to wait for my brother to wake up. I got up to his room, and Passion was lying in the chair with the baby. It was a little after eight so I sent her home with my Grams and Journey, who were waiting for me to come back. None of us were leaving him alone, and by the looks of things, he wouldn't be here that much longer. I cut the light off in his room and went to sleep. I woke up and saw this woman I swear was my mom standing at the door. I tried to get up, but I couldn't move. The person came closer to me, and it scared the fuck out of me because she was floating.

"Jax, that man is coming back for you, Journey, and Haven. You have to pay attention to your surroundings and some of the people you know."

"I miss you and dad, Ma. This shit is hectic out here."

"*I know, son, and we miss you too. I wish I could hold all three of you and my three grandbabies.*"

"*Three.*"

"*Yea, Journey is three months, and Haven just got that girl pregnant.*"

"*Really?*"

"*Yea. She loves him, and she's going to be good for him. Make sure you try and keep him on the straight and narrow. I know how hard-headed he is. And you and Journey can't hold onto the hurt that their brother did. They had nothing to do with it, and they were only trying to avenge his death like Haven did for us. All of you have to sit down and figure this out. It's not time for any of you to join me and your dad.*"

"*But Ma, this stuff that's going on is never going to end.*" Just as I said that, I saw another figure, and it was my dad.

"*Son, Freedom is the one who had Wolf shot, and he is Venus's father. The entire situation is complicated, but somehow, all of you will have to come together to take him down. His kids don't love him as much as you think they do. Remember that.*" They started fading away, and I felt my eyes watering.

"*Jax, WIPE THOSE TEARS. What do I always say?*"

"*Real men don't cry.*"

"*Exactly. When your brother gets up, he will want to go to war. Keep him levelheaded until you can come together with Freedom's kids and take him out. He has a lot of people in high places too. I love you son, and tell Journey and Wolf the same thing.*"

"*I don't want to go yet.*" My mom said with tears falling down her face.

"Ma, don't go."

"I have to, but know that I'm watching over you three and your father's crazy mother too. I love you three with all my heart. Be safe."

"Ma?! Ma?!" I found myself waking up, and Wolf was staring at me like I was crazy.

"What the fuck was you dreaming about?" He said trying to take the blood pressure cuff off.

"Mom and dad came to me in my dream." He stopped what he was doing and looked at me.

"Yea right."

"Did you know Journey was pregnant?" His silence gave me my answer.

"Who told you?"

"Ma did. She also told me you just got that chick pregnant." He snapped his neck to look and me and then winced in pain.

"I just slept with her. Damn it can happen that quick?"

"You idiot; it can happen the first time you nut in a woman. Are you ready for a kid?"

"Not really, but if it happens, then it is what it is. She is my girl now, so I guess it was fate."

"Come, again? Did my whoreish brother just say he had a girlfriend and not a fuck buddy?" I asked making both of us laugh.

"Yea man. She asked me, and I said yes. I know it was ass backwards, but I didn't even know she was interested."

"Man please. We all knew that chick loved you."

"Why does everyone keep saying that? I didn't know."

"You wouldn't if you're fucking everyone else."

"Man whatever. Yo, the dude that had me shot was-"

"Colby's father. I know." I cut him off.

"How?"

"I told you they came to me. I know it seems crazy because black people don't see ghosts, but remember, we're mixed, so maybe the white part of us allowed me to see them."

"Yo, I'm going to act like you didn't say no dumb shit like that. What else did they say?" I told him everything my dad said and how he wanted him to stay calm for a while. I also told him what went down with the Foster family too.

"I'm sorry man. Who knew you two would fall in love with his siblings? Fuck it; the way I see it is, they took two people from us, and I only took one. I feel like we're owed a body so whose it going to be?"

"Take your ass back to sleep, Wolf. Ain't nobody killing no one tonight." I said and laid back on the couch they had in his room. I thought about Venus until sleep finally found me.

Journey

Tonight was a complete nightmare, and all I wanted to do was wake up and realize it was a dream. After we got to the house from picking some things up for Passion and her son, Christian, I showed her to one of the guest rooms that she could sleep in. I took a shower and laid down in my bed. There was a knock at my door, and shockingly, it was Colby. I was surprised my grandmother allowed him in the house. He and I just stared at one another for a few minutes, then I stood up and walked over to where he was and jumped in his arms. I knew that, with everything going on, I should be mad at him, but my body was calling him, and I think he felt the same.

He kicked the door shut and laid me down on the bed. I sat up and removed his belt buckle, unzipped his jeans, and pulled his clothes down. I licked my lips as I stared at his dick standing at attention. I glanced up, and he was smiling at me; that alone made me want him more. I placed the tip in my mouth and flickered my tongue around the way he liked it. I used my lips to suck on it like a lollipop. I moved up and down his shaft feeling the tip touch the back of my throat. I made a humming sound and it vibrated making his body shake.

"Dammit, Journey. You're going to make me cum fast." I felt his hand moving around in my hair, while I let my tongue slide down until I made it to his balls, where I took each one in my mouth and played around with them.

"Yea baby. Make daddy cum for you." When he said that, I went back to sucking and jerking until I felt him allowing me to swallow his future kids. He pulled me up to him, put me on his shoulders, and ate my pussy so good I had to hold onto his shoulders to keep from falling. The minute he entered me, it was like we were one again and nothing could come between us. Every stroke felt like he was touching my stomach, as he hit spots that made me lose my breath.

"I love you so much, Journey, and I'm sorry about everything. Please don't leave me. I need you right now." He said and buried his head in my neck while he continued maneuvering in and out of his favorite place. "Fuckkkk baby. You feel so good." He moaned out when I slid down on top of him.

"I love you too baby. You're telling me not to leave you, but I hope you don't leave me. Oh my God, I'm cumming."

He pumped harder underneath me and held me tight as we both released at the same time. He sat up while he was still in me and held me close. I wrapped my arms around his neck and kissed him hungrily turning us both back on. After another sex session, we took a shower together and got in the bed, where he was hugging me like he never wanted to let go.

"Colby, why did all of this happen to us?"

"I don't know, baby, but I'm not about to let anyone hurt you. I have your heart, and I'm going to protect and cherish it like I was supposed to do the first time. Do you trust me?" At first, I wanted to say no because of everything that had happened prior to tonight, but I wasn't going to be petty.

"Yes. I know you love me, and believe it or not, I know you wouldn't hurt me on purpose." I turned over, and he was smiling down at me.

"You're going to be the mother of my kids, and I promise that you're going to be my wife."

"Don't you think that's a little too early to be thinking about?"

"I know what I want and who I want it with, and that's you. Nothing or no one is going to keep me from you again." He pressed his lips to mine, and I could feel him and myself becoming aroused again. His phone started going off, so he picked it up to see who it was.

"Yea, Wesley." He answered and I sat up. They started talking about something so I threw my robe on to go downstairs.

"You thirsty baby." I whispered in his ear and kissed his neck.

"Just for that pussy." He covered the phone before he said it.

"I'll get you a water for now." He shook his head and finished his conversation. I closed the door behind me and walked down the stairs slowly. I felt a little lightheaded, but it was probably because I needed something to drink. I went in the kitchen, and my grandmother was sitting at the table on her phone. She didn't look up so I went to see what she was doing, and as usual, she was playing one of those games. I grabbed two waters out the fridge and sat down at the table with her.

"Did you two make up?" She asked and put her phone down.

"Sort of."

"Girl, don't play with me. You know that man be having you screaming. I can hear you all the way down here."

"Grams. I can't with you."

"What? That man is handsome; he puts that ass to sleep, and Journey, he loves the hell out of you."

"I know, Grams, but I can't help but feel some kind of way about him not telling me that, that was his brother."

"Honey, he can't tell you something that he didn't know you were aware of. Now I'm not saying what your brother did was wrong when he killed him, but I understand why his siblings feel the way they do."

"I know but-"

"But nothing. You can't take out on him what his brother did to my son and your mother. He didn't know, and the way I look at it is no one got the good end of the stick.

You and your brothers lost your parents, I lost my son, and they lost their brother. There are no real winners here, but the love that man has for you should be enough to move past that."

"Thanks Grams." I stood up from the table and she stopped me.

"Ugh, don't forget that nigga lied and cheated though. I know you may be horny, and even though you made up, don't give him no more until you think he learned his lesson." I laughed at her and gave her a hug before I went back upstairs. I saw Passion coming out the room, and she ran over to me.

"Are you ok?"

"I'm fine. I'm just tired. Are you ok?" I repeated the same question to her.

"Yea. You know Wolf and I just made it official, and I was scared that I would lose him as fast as I got him." She wiped the tears that were falling.

"Passion, my brother is too evil to die, and he's not going to leave me or my brother on this earth without him. Now that you and your son are in his life, he's not going anywhere."

"I hope not."

"Girl, go to sleep so you can get up early to see him. If I know Wolf, he's already been up and asked to go home. That's why I was happy that Jax stayed with him. There was no way we would've been able to make him stay."

Tina J.

"Goodnight, Journey." She went back to the room, and I went into mine. I closed the door and put the water on the nightstand next to Colby who had fallen asleep. I ran my hand down his face and watched him sleep. He was everything I prayed for in a man, and I wasn't going to lose him to anyone. I kissed his cheek and walked back around the bed to lie down. I kept having these weird dizzy spells, and I know I should've waken him up or told my grandmother, but I didn't. There was so much going on, and I didn't want them to worry about me.

****

The next morning, I woke up, and Colby was coming out the bathroom. He had a towel wrapped around him, and the water was still on the upper half of his body. I watched him walk around to where I was and sit down on the bed. I wanted to get up, but again, I was too dizzy. He carried me in the bathroom and sat me down on the toilet. When I finished, I stood up and grabbed onto the sink. I wasn't in any pain, but I didn't like the feeling. It was like I was on a roller coaster or hung over.

"Babe, you ok in there?" I heard him yell out.

"I'm good." I leaned on the sink, picked up my toothbrush, and started brushing my teeth. I washed my face and turned around to find him standing behind me grinning.

"You are beautiful, and I can't wait to see you walk down the aisle."

"Colby, you are silly. We're not engaged, and that's a long way from now."

"I can dream, can't I? And we'll be engaged soon enough." He pecked my lips and grabbed my hand to go back in the room.

"Are you ok?" He stood in front of me and stared into my eyes.

"Yea. I think I'm getting sick."

"Let me take you to the doctor."

"No baby. I'm good. Go handle your business, and I'll see you later." I told him hoping he was ok with that.

"Nah, I'm staying here with you. All that other shit can wait."

"Colby, I'm ok. I promise. I'm going to take a shower and get back in the bed."

"Fine. I'm going to stay here until you're done." He helped me in the shower and stood there watching me wash up. I saw concern on his face, but he didn't say anything. I wrapped the towel around me, then he lifted me up, took me back into the room, and sat me on the chaise. He put lotion on my body and rubbed deodorant on me. I told him what pajamas I wanted to wear, and he dressed me in them.

"Yo Grams. Can you come up here?" I heard him ask as he put slippers on my feet. He started making the bed and handed me my cell phone.

"What your big headed ass want? And what's wrong with her?"

"You see it too right?"

"Journey, what is it?" She rushed to my side and felt my forehead.

"Nothing Grams. I was just feeling dizzy and your grandson-in-law started worrying. I'm fine."

"She won't let me take her to the doctor, and I'm not leaving her like this."

"If you have something to do, go ahead Colby. I'll be here with her."

"I'm good. I'm not leaving her."

"Colby, Grams will be here. If I go to the doctor, you will be the first person she calls." He looked at my grandmother, and she nodded her head yes. He lifted me up and took me downstairs to lay on the couch. He said I didn't need to be up there in case I had to leave. It was too many steps, and I could fall. I think he was more worried than I was. After he kissed me, he made sure I had my cell phone and charger before he left. My Grams made me some eggs and bacon to eat. She thought that maybe me not eating was the reason I was dizzy.

After I ate, I started to feel a little better, so my Grams had me sit outside on the porch. The summer breeze felt good as we sat out there talking about what's been going on. Passion ended up coming outside with Christian and told us she was on her way up to the hospital, because Wolf was awake and wanted to see them. I was proud of my brother for at least trying to be a boyfriend. All of this was new to him, so it was going to be funny to watch.

Passion said her goodbyes, and Grams and I decided to go out to eat for lunch. We sat in the Olive Garden eating the house salad that I couldn't get enough of when I saw Colby's ex walk in with an older gentlemen. She was limping a little, and the guy she was with acted like he could care less. He sat down without helping her and had a scowl on his face. His eyes locked with mine, and he blew me a kiss. I saw Willow turn around and roll her eyes. I told my grandmother, and once she turned around, shit hit the fan. I ran after her, but I wasn't fast enough.

"You killed my son, her mother, and tried to take out my grandson. I see now that you want a war, and if that's what you want, that's what you'll have."

"I see you're the same bitter bitch from back in the day. Is that pussy still good though?" My mouth dropped open when he said that. "Let me guess. You miss the way I had you moaning out my name." He had a sneaky grin on his face.

"You can say that." His father said smirking.

"Freedom, you need to stop this bullshit you got going on. You're going to miss out on meeting your grandkids." He looked over at me.

"So my son knocked up the sister of the man who killed his brother Dice. I see good pussy runs in that family." I was disgusted by what he was saying, but Willow was getting a kick out of it.

"I guess it does because your son can't seem to get enough of it." I gave that bitch a fake smile, and she rolled her eyes. My grandmother tossed a drink on him, and we went back to sit down. I was ready to go, but my stomach not being full wouldn't allow me to. We finished our meal, and on our way out, my grandmother flipped him the bird, and his nasty ass flickered his tongue between his two fingers.

When we got to the car, me and my grandmother busted out laughing. She started telling me how she was sleeping with him all the way up until Dice killed my parents. She thought they were in love, but he couldn't have been, because he never would've killed her only son. The two stopped speaking, and today was the first time they saw each other in years.

"Wait, I thought he was still with their mom."

"She left him after they had Venus. He cheated on her a lot, and it took a toll on her. When she found out she had cancer, the kids spent more and more time with her, but when Dice died, she blamed him. I think his death is what really killed her. No parent wants to bury their child." I nodded my head, because as an expectant mother, I couldn't imagine that.

We pulled up at the house, and Jax was there eating some leftovers that were in the fridge. He told us Venus left him, and I gave him a hug. When he told me the dream he had about my mom and dad, I started crying. I missed them so much and wished they were here. After he left, Grams and I locked up and went into our rooms.

My baby: *How are you feeling? I miss you.*

The text from Colby said when I looked down on my phone. He had been checking on me all day.

Me: *I'm a lot better. I miss you too, Am I going to see you tonight?*

My baby: *Of course. You want me to come to you.*

Me: *Yea. It's after nine, and I'm in the bed already.*

My baby: *Ok. I'll see you soon. I love you.*

Me: *I love you too. If I'm sleep when you get here, wake me up.*

My baby: *Ok.*

I put the phone down and fell asleep. I have no idea when Colby got there, but I felt him behind me, and that's all that mattered.

Colby

The shit that happened a couple of weeks ago didn't do anything but bring Journey and I closer. Those dizzy spells she had were getting worse. She thought I didn't notice it, but I found myself doing a lot of shit from her house or making her come to mine. I wanted to make sure nothing happened to her, and if it did, I was right there to get her to the hospital. I spoke with a doctor, and he said that her symptoms can be from her being pregnant, but it could also be something else. I tried to get her to go to the hospital, but she wouldn't. I was happy today was her four-month mark, and that she had a doctor's appointment. I helped her out the car and walked into the doctor's office with her. I had her going to a private doctor, because that urgent care place wasn't for her. She only went that day, because it was the only one that could get her in quickly.

Journey sat down in the waiting room while I picked up the clipboard to fill out the information. The stuff I didn't know, she put down, and I took it up to the desk. The nurse came out ten minutes later and escorted us to the back. She had her vitals done, and the nurse told her to lie on the table, unbutton her pants, and pull them down. She gave her a piece of paper that was supposed to be like a blanket to cover her. The doctor came in, and Journey gave her an update on how she'd been feeling, but I noticed she left out the dizzy spells. I had no problem relaying the information to her. Journey cut her eyes at me, but I didn't care.

"You hungry?" I asked her after we left the doctor's office. She nodded her head yes and I pulled up at Chili's.

"Baby, I think something is wrong." She said when I got to her side of the car to open the door. I looked at her, and she was sweating and her eyes were rolling. I closed the door and ran back to get in the driver's side. I called her grandmother and told her to meet us at the hospital.

"Journey, stay awake baby." I was shaking her gently, and she kept asking me to stop. It seemed like it took me forever to get there. Once we made it, I saw her grandmother and Wolf's girlfriend coming out. I was hoping her brothers weren't here, because I wasn't in the mood for no shit. I hadn't seen or spoken to them since that day.

I jumped out the car and carried her in the door, and both of her brothers were standing right there. The nurses all sprang into action and asked me to take her to the back and lay her on the stretcher. Her eyes weren't rolling anymore, but she was still sweating, and she was burning up. The doctor came running in, and I was given another clipboard to fill out information.

"Yo, what the fuck are you doing?" I yelled out when I saw one of the nurses jabbing her arm with a needle. Journey was crying, and the sight was breaking my heart. I had to be escorted out, because I wouldn't leave them alone with her. I was scared they were going to fuck up. I walked past her brothers, and we just ice grilled each other. No one knew Journey and I were back together except her grandmother, and we wanted to keep it that way for now, but at this moment, I gave zero fucks, and if they wanted it, they could get it. I was standing outside talking to Venus who hadn't spoken to Journey or Jax either. She was crying hysterically, because she felt bad.

"Are you ok, Colby?" I turned around, and it was her grandmother. This woman was funny as hell, and she always kept it real with me. I looked at her like she was my own grandmother since both of mine passed away. She gave me a hug, and it felt good to have someone there understand what I was going through.

"I just want to know what's wrong with her. I can't lose her again." I felt a tear leaving my face and wiped it before she saw it, but I was too late.

"Don't be ashamed to show emotions for the woman you love."

"I'm not. I don't want her to see me like this, because she'll be worried about me instead of herself."

"You're right about that. What happened?" I explained everything to her, and she nodded her head. She asked if Journey was bleeding. I told her no, and she was happy about that. We walked back in, and I sat there for what seemed like hours waiting to hear what was wrong with her. The chick Passion stood up and said goodbye, and that Journey will be fine. I told her thank you and leaned my head back on the wall. Her brothers were on the other side of the waiting room talking but stopped when Venus and Wesley walked in. Jax and Venus couldn't stop staring at each other, but Wesley pushed her towards me.

"We're supposed to be here for Colby, and you're staring at your ex." I could hear Wesley saying to her.

"Shut up. That's the second time I've seen him since we found out about Dice."

"That's your fault. We told you to go back to him, but you rather pout and make everybody else miserable around you." She and Wesley went back and forth making me laugh.

"You think this shit is funny? My sister is laid up in the hospital, and everything is a joke to you." Wolf said coming towards us. Wesley and I pushed Venus behind us and stood up.

"Nigga, fuck out of here with that shit. You may have these niggas out here on the streets scared of you, but you pump no fear over here."

"Is that right?"

"That's exactly right. That may be your sister in there, but that's my fucking girl, and she's carrying my seed. My family came to support me and said some funny shit, and if I want to laugh, I can. Get the fuck out of here with that bullshit."

"Oh you tough." Wolf said and stepped into my personal space.

"Tough enough. I'm saying; it's obvious you got a problem, and it ain't nothing to go outside and handle it."

"Nah, we can handle it right here." This nigga pulled out his gun and shot me in the leg. I took my gun out and did the same shit to him. There wasn't a loud noise since we both had silencers. Neither one of us dropped and stood there staring each other down. The crazy part is no one said a word.

"That's all you got nigga. We can keep going." He said, and I heard the doctor come out asking for Journey's family.

"Doctor, I'm her grandmother. How is she?" I wanted to turn and go over there, but he was still in my face.

"But the both of them need to be looked at." The doctor said staring down at both of us bleeding.

"Oh, those dumb niggas just shot each other. They'll be ok. How is my grandbaby?" I fell back on the chair, and Venus asked the nurse to come help me. I tried listening to the doctor, but I couldn't hear him.

"We'll finish this another time my nigga." He said as the nurse wheeled him to the back.

"I'll be waiting motherfucker." I told him, and they took me in a different direction.

I don't know how long I was there, but when I woke up, my father was sitting in the chair next to my bed, and Willow was with him. She stood up and came to kiss me, but I turned my head. Willow nodded at my father, and he got up and walked out. I heard the door close behind him. I threw the covers back and limped to the bathroom.

"You can follow behind my pops and leave too." I said and closed the door. "What the hell is going on?" I came out the bathroom and pushed Willow to the floor when she got on her knees trying to put her hand under my hospital gown.

"You're father wants me to have a baby with you."

"WHAT? Hell no." I said as she started undressing. She went on and on about how they saw my girl in the Olive Garden, and he found out he was going to be a grandfather and how most likely he would never get the chance to meet my child. She climbed on top of the bed and started trying to suck my dick.

"Willow, get up now." I was trying to be as calm as possible.

"Colby. You always had the best dick. Well, you and Wolf, but neither of you want to fuck me again, so it looks like I'm going to have to take it. She went back to trying, and I pushed her dumb ass off the bed. The stuff my father was going through made no sense.

"Stop acting like you don't miss me." She said and sat on the chair with her legs cocked open. I picked the remote up and ignored the hell out of her. She didn't turn me on, and being in as much pain as I was in, there was no use in physically trying to remove her, so I let her continue while I watched TV.

"Why don't you let me have your baby? No one has to know."

"Bitch, are you crazy?"

"Colby, I made them bring me to you." I heard Journey's voice as the door opened, and the hurt that was etched on her face as she stood there staring at a naked Willow was going to haunt me. I tried to get out the bed.

"Journey, it's not what it looks like?"

"Colby, you promised." She said, and I saw her eyes getting watery.

"What can I say? I have better pussy than you." Willow said, and I wanted to smack the shit out of her.

"Yea right, Willow. Journey, I swear I didn't want this. I woke up, and she and my father were sitting in here. Baby, she took her clothes off, but I didn't touch her." The nurse had her face turned up at Willow.

"Colby, stop lying. You asked me to suck your dick, and afterwards, you were going to fuck me so you could get me pregnant."

"Bitch, stop lying." I threw the tissue box at her and tried to throw the hospital phone at her. My leg was in so much pain, and when I tried to jump out the bed, I almost fell. I think the stitches popped, because there was blood on my leg.

"Journey, I wouldn't lie to you, and I damn sure wouldn't cheat on you again. Willow, I swear you better go into hiding, because when I get out of here, you're as good as dead." I saw Journey say something to the nurse, then the nurse turned her around and started taking her out the room.

"Journey, don't leave. JOURNEY?!" I yelled out after her. *I can't fucking win for losing.*

My father walked back in the room a few minutes after Journey left and asked Willow how it went. I couldn't believe he was doing this. I heard Willow tell him she should've done it while I was still sleeping off the anesthesia, because I wouldn't have fought her. I think these motherfuckers have lost their minds.

"Yo, you'll really do some shit like this to me, Pops. I get why you want to get at Wolf, but why do you want her to hurt?"

"Because Journey is their pride and joy. They will be upset if Wolf dies, but it will be a fucking tragedy if she does."

"Pops, how do you think I'm going to feel? She's carrying my child, your grandbaby, and I'm going to marry her one day. You don't think the shit you doing is hurting me or don't you care because I'm not Dice?"

"I wish it were you or Wesley that died. The only thing I wish came from this is that Dice killed all of them. Dice was much tougher than you, and that bitch would've been dead a long time ago." I saw the way Willow looked at my dad. It was like she felt bad for me because he said that. I pressed the nurses' button and asked them to have security escort them out. I was over trying to figure out what was going on in his head.

****

36

The next two days, I laid in the hospital and asked them to put me under a different name. I wanted everyone to think I left. They allowed me to leave a couple of days later, so I went home to grab some clothes and checked into a hotel. I had too much shit going on, and I needed time to myself. I wanted to call Journey, but I knew she didn't want to hear from me. I had to come up with a plan and fast to get rid of my father and get my girl back.

Venus

Colby called and told me something was wrong with Journey, and I instantly felt like shit. I alienated myself from her too when I found out Wolf was the one who killed my brother. I may not fuck with my dad, but me and my brother Dice were close. He used to help me with my homework and take me anywhere I wanted to go. When he died, I attached myself to Colby, who was always quiet and never wanted to be caught up in my dad's shit. Unfortunately, when Colby got to a certain age, my dad forced killing on him.

At first, Colby fought him every step of the way, but he eventually went along with it. My mom hated my dad when Dice died and said that Colby would get the same fate if he put him out there, and now look. The woman he was in love with had a brother that shot him in the hospital. The entire scene was crazy, but all I found myself doing was staring at Jax, who was staring at me.

I texted him a week before the incident at the hospital and told him that we had a doctor's appointment. When we were there, I started getting jealous because he paid more attention to his phone than he did me. I know I told him it was over, but secretly, I wanted him to fight harder for me. Wesley and Colby both told me I was stupid. What Dice and Wolf did shouldn't reflect on our relationship, but me being the stubborn bitch I am, allowed it to. The doctor asked if we wanted to know what we were having, and I didn't answer but he told her yes. When she announced it was a boy, he started smiling. I knew that's what he wanted so I was happy for him. I went behind the shade to put my clothes on and made plans to talk to him, but he was gone when I finished.

Tonight, there was a party at the strip club he owned and a few of the women that came in the shop were going. I wasn't going to go, but hell, I was tired of sitting in the house. I threw on a pair of maternity jeans that looked more like regular ones and put a nice cream sweater on and some black shoes. My hair was already done, so I didn't have to worry about that. I wasn't speaking to Journey, and she was my only friend, so I was riding solo to the club, and I hope no one noticed.

I stepped in the club and it was beyond packed. I sat at the bar, for what, I don't know, because I couldn't drink. I looked around and didn't see Jax anywhere. I finally said fuck it and went to see if he was in his office.

"Aww shit, Jax. This dick is real good." I opened his office door, and that's all I heard the girl say as she rode him in the chair. I wasn't sure if she was a stripper, and at this moment, I didn't care. I yanked her back by her hair and started punching her in the face. I felt someone lifting me up and turned around to see my ex standing there with no shirt on. His body was still amazing, and I wanted to have him next

40

to me tonight when I went to bed, but I knew that wasn't happening.

"Are you stupid? You're pregnant and you come up in my shit fighting someone I'm fucking."

"Jax, how could you?"

"How could I what Venus? You said it was over, and I waited for you to stop being stubborn and find your way back, but you didn't. What? Did you think I was going to wait around for you?"

"Well yea."

"You have to be the dumbest bitch I know if you thought that."

"That's what it's come to Jax? You're calling me bitches now."

"Bitch, I'm about to fuck you up." The other chick said.

Phew.

Was all I heard and she hit the floor. I looked at her and shook my head. I was surrounded by nothing but savages, and maybe it was better to leave him alone.

"Why did you shoot her?"

"She should've never said she was going to lay hands on you. I don't care who I'm with, you're my son's mother, and no one will be threatening or putting their hands on you. And you're not a bitch, I said you were acting like one." He said and walked to his desk. I went to leave, and he stopped me.

"Venus." I turned around praying he wanted me to stay.

"Yea."

"Don't come back here."

"Huh?"

"Don't bring you ass back to this club. You are no longer my girl, and I don't owe you shit, so don't stand there looking for an explanation. You did this." He said pointing to the dead chick. "If you have anyone to blame for getting what used to be your dick, blame yourself." All I could do was shake my head. He was right; had I not been stubborn and had listened to him when he wanted to talk, or been there when he needed me, we would still be together. I walked out the club feeling defeated and went to my car. I noticed a couple of black Suburban's pull up and watched as they got out the car around the corner. I called Jax up over and over until he answered. He may have just let me have it but I wasn't going to allow anyone to kill him either.

"WHAT Venus?" He yelled in the phone.

"Jax, I just wanted to tell you that a couple of Suburban's pulled up on the side of the club, and they are putting on vests."

"How many?"

"I don't know."

"Take your ass home. I'll handle it." Was all he said and disconnected the call? I wanted to stay, but I couldn't take the chance of getting caught in the crossfire. I called Colby up, and he told me he was at Wesley's house and to stop by. I was disgusted when I got there and saw that they were having a party. Women were walking around half naked, and there were drinks and food on the table and counters.

"I want some of that dick baby." Some chick said feeling on my brother's dick. He was smiling as he drank something out the cup. I pushed her back and pulled him to the side. I took him into the bathroom and shut the door.

"What are you doing? Journey is going to kick your ass."

"Where you been? I haven't heard or seen her since I left the hospital and that shit went down with Willow. Journey will always have a place in my heart, but I'm done fighting with her. I tried to explain what happened and she wasn't trying to hear it. I don't blame her because I fucked up before."

"So what? You're just going to be out here fucking random bitches?"

"Pretty much." He said pulling out a row of condoms. I smacked him on the arm.

"What's up with you and Jax?"

"Nothing. I just caught him fucking some bitch at the club in his office."

"Damnnnnnnn. He was doing it like that?"

"Yup. I beat her up, she threatened me, and then he killed her." I told him, and he almost spilled his drink laughing.

"Stop laughing."

"I can't. That nigga killed a bitch for threatening you. I can see if she put hands on you. That man still loves you if he's killing for you."

"No. He said it's because I'm his son's mother, and that's the only reason why?"

"Wow. I'm having a nephew?"

"Yup. When does Journey find out?"

"Next week."

"Are you going to the appointment?"

"Hell yea. She can be mad all she wants, but that's my baby in there, and I ain't missing no doctors' visit because she wants to believe that shit with Willow." I felt bad for my brother. He told me what my father and Willow did, and I hated him even more for that shit.

I couldn't stand my father, because I blamed him for my brother getting killed. I also blamed him for getting Colby and Wesley mixed up in his line of work. Wesley was my father's son by a woman he cheated on my mother with. That was another reason I didn't like him. He cheated on my mom horribly, and each time, she took him back. That's why I was scared to love Jax, because I didn't want him to cheat on me, and I take him back. I loved my mom to death, but she was weak for my dad, and it made me sick watching it take place. He and I got into a hundred arguments, but the last one we had a few years ago made him cut me off and I said fuck him.

"Can I stay at your house? I don't want to go home."

"You got your key?"

"Yea. And don't bring no hoes home with you."

"Hell no. I'm fucking these bitches right here in our hoe house." I laughed because this really was the place Wesley was at all the time, but it wasn't his home.

"Bitches."

"Yup. That chick you pushed came with two friends, and they all want to feel me inside them. You think I'm turning that shit down. You must be crazy."

"Boy move."

"Aye." I turned around.

"Ain't no boy over here."

"Shut up and take those nasty hoes upstairs."

"You ain't said nothing but a word sis. Love you and send me a text when you get to the house." I told him ok and headed for the door. I looked back, and the same chick I moved was walking in front of him up the steps, while the other two were behind him. Women had no respect for themselves nowadays.

I pulled up at Colby's house and took my bag out that I picked up from my house on the way over. I was lonely there, and my aunt, uncle, and cousins were still visiting and they were staying with my brother. At least, if I stayed over here, I would have someone to talk to. I went to the room I always stayed in and locked the door. I started the bath and waited for it to fill up. I stepped inside and laid back thinking about

Jax. It's been a minute since I've felt him, and I was horny, but he told me to my face not to come back around him.

I stayed in the tub for a half hour, and when I got out, my body was wrinkled as hell. I put lotion and my pajamas on and got in the bed. I turned the news on and there was a massive shooting outside of Club Jax. There were some fatalities and a lot of injuries. I wanted to text Jax and see if he was ok, but a text came through from him before I was able to.

Jax: *You are probably sleep but I wanted to say thank you for the heads up and that I'm ok.*

I didn't respond to the text but I did go to bed happy knowing he was safe. I'm not sure who sent the people to the club, but I can bet it was most likely my father. There was about to be a war, and I prayed that everyone I loved made it out alive.

Wolf

"Shit baby, I'm cumming again." Passion moaned in my ear as I had her legs over my shoulders to reach deeper. In the beginning, she couldn't take it all, but once she got used to it, she had been handling it like a pro. I felt her let go on me and came not too long after her. This was our third session for the night, and we were both ready to go to sleep.

I walked into the bathroom and put some soap on a rag to wash us both up. I had moved her and Christian in with me when I was released from the hospital the second time. My house had cameras, and it was in the cut where no one knew except my family. I washed both of us up and laid in the bed next to her. Passion and I had been official for over a month now. I thought it was going to be hard being a one-woman man, but it wasn't. Then again, I didn't hang out in the club as much, so the temptation wasn't there.

"You know you're pregnant right?" I said to her as she put her head on my chest.

"All the sex we have, I'm sure I am. Do you want me to get rid of it?" I lifted her head up to look at me.

"Do you want to?" I was a firm believer in allowing a woman to make the decision about her body.

"No, but we haven't been together long and-" I shushed her with a kiss on the lips.

"I want whatever you want."

"If it's a boy, do we have to name him Wolf, Jr?"

"Hell yea. What you think this is? I have to have a legacy."

"He can be named after you, but Wolf is a nickname."

"Exactly. One that he'll have." She laughed.

I turned the television on and started flipping through the channels. I stopped at the news when I saw a place that looked like my brother's club. I picked my phone up, but his shit kept going to voicemail. I turned the T.V. up and listened to the reporters say that there were multiple fatalities and injuries. I was going to call Venus, but he told me that they hadn't spoken in a while. He only saw her at the doctors' appointments. I called Journey up, and she cursed me out because she was asleep. Her ass woke right up when I told her about the club, though. She told me she would meet me down there, but I told her ass to stay in the house, and that I would call her when I knew something.

"Be careful baby." Passion said and kissed me before I left.

I sped to the club, and when I got there, it was mad cops and ambulances out there. I didn't see Jax, but it could be that he wasn't there... I hoped he wasn't anyway. I stepped past one of the cops when he wasn't paying attention and went inside. There were people being treated at the bar, but no dead bodies inside though. I ran upstairs to his office, and he was coming out the bathroom.

"Yo why weren't you answering your phone?"

"Oh shit. My bad. The battery died. How did you hear about it?" He plugged his phone into the charger.

"Nigga. The news people are outside."

"Shit, let me text Journey and Venus."

"Venus."

"Yes, Venus."

"I thought you two weren't speaking." He proceeded to tell me everything that went down. He also told me she was the one that gave him a heads up on the Suburbans. I sat down listening to him tell me that, whoever sent them made sure they wore vests and that they bombarded their way through the door when the club was letting out. That was weird, because everyone knew we never came out the front. That's when he told me that they had all the entrances covered. He and Drew had our people come up there, and that's why shit got out of hand. Our people were just like us and had no problem killing anyone, anywhere.

"Venus didn't text me back. Maybe she didn't see it."

"Yo, if you want your girl back, go get her."

"Nah. When I needed her, she turned her back on me. Even after I found that shit out, and they came for you in the hospital, I was still willing to be with her, but she said fuck me."

"Yea man, but she was going through something."

"And so was I. So was Journey, but her and that nigga stayed together. I don't know what's going on with them now, but shit, they got through it. Venus was being stubborn, and when I needed her the most, she bailed. I can't and won't go through that shit every time she gets mad." I understood what he was saying.

"What happened with Journey and that stupid nigga?"

"Man, the shit funny as hell." I sat back in my chair laughing hard as hell when he told me the great lengths his father went through to get him to sleep with his ex. I felt bad for Journey, because she walked in on it and believed the chick, but I would find it hard to see anything different if I walked in on that too.

"Who the hell told you?"

"Willow must've told someone, and one of the strippers came to the office and told me."

"Was that before or after you fucked her?" He gave me the side eye.

"Nigga, please. Now that you're a free man, and all this pussy is in your face, I know you've been trying it."

"I fucked her after." He busted out laughing.

"I knew it."

"What? I had to thank her for the information and told her I better not hear it repeated.

"I hope you're strapping up with these bitches."

"Oh, hell yea. Ain't no one having my seeds but Venus."

"But y'all ain't together."

"I don't give a fuck. When I want another kid, I'll fuck her raw and continue until she tells me she's pregnant again."

"Yo, that's straight savage shit."

"It takes one to know one."

"You're right." He and I sat in the office talking until the cops came up and told us everything was done. I didn't get home until almost six in the morning. I was happy that Passion wasn't a nagging woman. I called her when I first got here and told her that I was, most likely, staying with Jax. She told me ok, and that she was going to sleep. I pulled into the driveway and went into the house. I was tired as hell and wanted to lay up under my woman. I went in the room, and Christian and her were both knocked out in the bed. I moved him to the middle and got under the covers with them. My ass didn't get up until after two, and both of them were gone by then. Passion sent me a text saying she left my breakfast in the microwave and that she loved me.

I handled my hygiene and went downstairs to eat. Then, I picked my phone up and got the confirmation that the people from the farm were going to bring the pony and some other nasty ass animals to Christian's party. He was turning one, and Passion wanted to give him a party at Chucky Cheese, but I told her ass hell no, and that we would have one at the community center, because they had a huge area where the kids could play outside and those animals could roam. Plus, I wasn't having anyone from her family or his father's coming to my house. I didn't trust no one. I went by Journey's house when I got dressed and saw that she was sitting outside.

"What up sis?"

"Nothing bro."

"When do you find out what you're having?"

"Ugh tomorrow." She said like she was aggravated by the question.

"Why you say it like that?"

"Because I have to see him at the appointment." I started laughing and laid down in one of the chairs next to her.

"Journey, that man loves you. He went to great lengths to get you back in his life after he fucked up. Do you honestly think he would cheat on you again? Think about it. He went to war with his father over you, shot his ex over you, most likely cried over you." She pushed me in the arm.

"What? I'm serious. You yourself said that he wanted you to move in and marry him. Why would he go through all that if he wanted to be with someone else? I can see if you were living with him and married, because by then, he had you." I looked over at her, and she was crying.

"Haven, I love him so much, but when I saw his ex standing there naked, all I saw was him cheating on me. I thought they were playing sex games. Then, she was naked and saying he was lying, and I didn't know who to believe."

"Always believe your man before you believe a woman who wants him. Mom used to tell me when I got older that, when I found "the one" not to cheat on her, and if I did, then tell her before anyone else could, because people will always add fuel to the fire. She also said the woman I found should know she is always number one in my life and will never question me about what another one says."

"Do you feel like you were number one in his life?" I asked her as she wiped her eyes.

"From the very first day we met."

"Then there should have never been doubt. Once you took him back, it was supposed to be a clean slate for you, but you allowed that same woman, who has been a pain in the ass, force you to lose your man. You know she's probably been trying to fuck him ever since."

"Do you think he slept with her?" She asked me like I'm supposed to know the answer to that shit.

"I don't know sis, but you can't be mad if he did. You left him alone and pushed him back into the single world when all he wanted was you."

"Why are you on his side all of a sudden?"

"Honestly sis, I saw how in love he was with you when I stepped to him at the hospital. He didn't back down and went to bat over you with me. Hell, we shot each other and still made plans to get it popping. No other nigga in their right mind has ever gone against me."

"I love him, Haven, but-"

"There should be no buts. If you love him, then go get him." I told her, and she nodded her head. She laid her head on my shoulder, and we both sat out there for a while listening to nature. I didn't realize how long we were out there until Grams came out saying somebody better come eat her food because she didn't cook for nothing. The two of us got up and went to make a plate.

****

"I'm upstairs baby." I heard Passion yell out when I walked into the house. I left Journey's house right after I ate. I was still tired from being out all night.

"Da Da." I heard Christian call out, and I picked him up. I didn't correct him, because he was still a baby. I was his father as of right now since his was deceased. I never told Passion what happened to him, and she never asked. I think she knew, and she knew my policy for don't ask because I'm telling you shit.

"Congratulations, Daddy." She said, smiling and showing me the pregnancy test.

"Thanks baby."

"For what?" She said looking confused.

"For letting my wild ass seed grow in your belly. Just be ready for the pain, because I didn't plant no punks inside you."

"I can't with you." She tossed the test in the garbage and washed her hands.

"I'm serious. I love you, Passion, and I'm glad you're keeping it."

"You love me, Haven." I moved back when she said my name.

"What I tell you about that shit? But yes, I do love you." Christian started clapping his hands.

"I love you, too, lil man."

"That means I can get pussy for the next eight months without worrying about your period."

"Only you would think about that. Move with your crazy ass."

****

The next few days seemed to fly by, and today was Christian's party. I hired an event planner to set the center up so Passion didn't have too much to do. I kept Christian with me while she went to the salon and let Venus get her right. I told her Venus wouldn't be there too much longer, because she was getting bigger. She told me Venus told her she would do her hair at the house. I asked Passion did she want to quit Wal-Mart and be a stay at home mom, but she told me no; she would be bored. She didn't know yet, but she was going to be running the shop while Venus was out. She was going to find out today, and starting Monday, she will be going there to learn everything.

The party was in full swing, and there was a lot of kids there. Passion's nosy ass sister, Darlene, was there telling everyone in the hood's business. I noticed some familiar faces from the hood walk in but didn't say anything. Jax and Drew both made eye contact with me. I saw one of the women walk over to Passion, and they looked like they were in a heated argument. I asked Darlene who she was, and she said it was Christian's grandmother on his father's side. I saw how watery my girl's eyes were getting, and I didn't like that shit.

"What's the problem shorty?" I pulled Passion in front of me, and the lady turned her face up and folded her arms. She didn't even allow my girl to answer before she started trying to snap.

"The problem is my son has been missing for a while, and she is carrying on with this party like he don't mean shit." I had to chuckle before I responded.

"He don't mean shit. Not with her, he doesn't."

"What the fuck type of shit is that?"

"Passion, I think Christian is ready to cut his cake. You want to go get everything ready, and I'll be over there in a minute."

"Thanks baby."

"You know I got you." She kissed my lips and rolled her eyes at the woman.

"Listen, bitch."

"Bitch?"

"Yes, bitch. This party is for your grandson, and instead of you asking her where your loser ass son is, why don't you take your ass over there and say hello to him. The minute you walked in here, you came straight to my girl talking shit. If that's the reason you came here, you can walk out the same way you came in."

"Listen here, little nigga." The bitch had the nerve to put her finger in my face. I broke that shit and grabbed another one and broke that too. She looked down at her hand and then back at me. I smirked and finished saying what I had to say.

"Don't ever come somewhere I'm at and think you disrespecting me, or anyone I know, will be tolerated. I'm not sure if you're familiar with who I am, but you need to ask someone. I'm that nigga Wolf, and this ain't what you want." I saw her eyes pop open when I said that shit, then I began to escort her to the front.

"I think it's best for you to leave. Don't you?" She nodded her head yes.

"Now Passion won't be hearing from you anymore will she?"

"No." She had tears coming down her face.

"The hood talks you know that right?" She nodded her head up and down.

"If I hear you discussing my girl, her son, or what happened at this party, you see those two teenage kids you brought with you. They'll be taking a dirt nap. Now, get the fuck out of here." She walked away from me fast as hell.

"Did you handle that for me?"

"You don't even have to ask."

"Good. I promise to handle that for you later. I love you."

"You better, and I love you too. Now let's get some cake."

We walked over to where everyone was and sang Happy Birthday. Christian wasn't beat for all that yelling and jumped out of Passion's arms and into mine. After the singing was done, he still wasn't trying to hear leaving me. The only one he would go to was Journey, and it was probably because she was pregnant. I saw Venus walk in, and she instantly caught an attitude when she saw the chick Jax brought sitting on his lap. Oh well. She was the one who left him, and now she had to deal with her choices. I can finally say I'm glad I don't have to deal with that shit anymore.

After we finished cleaning up I dropped Passion off at home and told her I would be back in an hour or so. I picked Drew up because Jax had his hands full with Venus and the chick he came with. We drove to the hood in one of our hoopty's and it just so happened the person I was looking for was standing on the porch talking. I'm not sure about what but when she finished we watched her go inside and the person leave. I handed the blunt back to Drew and unlocked the door to get out. There weren't too many people outside but we still made sure not too draw too much attention.

"Who is it? I heard when Drew knocked on the door.

"Drew." His dumb ass answered like she would know who he was. The person opened the door without looking and literally pissed on herself when she saw me. I pushed the door open and we made our way inside. The house was filthy and it seemed like she lived alone.

"Yo, where are the two teenagers you had with you?"

"Those were my nieces. They went home after we left."

"Hmm." Drew and I both checked the house and he made sure the front door was closed.

"What are you doing here? I didn't say anything." She asked nervously.

"I'm sure you didn't. However, a nigga don't trust you." I saw her eyes get big. Drew grabbed a chair from the kitchen and brought it in the living room and pushed her down on it.

"This is what's going to happen." She shook her head no as the tears rolled down her eyes.

"What are you crying for I haven't even done anything yet." Drew was in the kitchen looking in her refrigerator.

"Damn bitch. Where's your food or even water? I should kill your ass myself for not having food in here." Drew was funny as hell. Anytime we ran up in somebody's shit the first thing he did was look in their fridge.

"Please don't hurt me."

"Oh now you're scared. You came to my son's party talking big shit to my girl. You hurt her feelings and no one hurts anyone close to me without feeling my wrath. So like I said here's what's going to happen." I screwed the silencer on my gun and continued talking.

"You're going to call my girl and apologize for the way you treated her today."

"But."

"But nothing. Just do it." She grabbed her phone with her good hand and asked for Passion's number. I forgot her loser son kept her cell phone and she didn't have a way to contact my girl. I gave it to her and made her put the phone on speaker. After she apologized she hung the phone up.

"Now don't you feel better." She nodded her head yes.

"I do too. Tell your son I said what's up." I let two shots off in her head.

"Dammit Wolf. I said let me kill her." Drew said coming out the bathroom.

"Man shut up. You in this motherfucker bitching because she aint have no food. Bring your ass on." After Drew set the house on fire I closed the door and watched it burn slowly. The two of us argued all the way back to the car about me shooting her. I told him next time I promise he could do it. This nigga was still trying to catch up to my body count. We lit another blunt and watched as the fire trucks and police came flying past us when we pulled off. I dropped him off at home and went to my house.

"I don't have to worry about her anymore." She said not looking up from the magazine she was reading.

"I'm taking a shower. Are you joining me." I completely ignored what she said.

"Haven." She said my name and I stepped in the bathroom. She never came in the shower with me but she waited for me to get in the bed before she spoke.

"I'm sorry. I forgot the policy of "Don't ask because you won 't tell me shit." Thank you for always protecting me and Christian. I love you." She said and scooted closer to me in the bed.

"I will always protect you. That's something you never have to worry about and I love you too. Good night." I put my arm around her and took my ass to sleep.

Jax

I noticed Venus when she walked in the party, and I also saw how she looked at the woman on my lap. I gave her the look that she better not start any shit. I watched her go over to Passion and hand her a bag that had a gift in it. She looked beautiful pregnant. I was going to speak, but there was no need when I was with someone. The party was winding down, and I noticed how she stayed to herself the entire time she was there. I don't think my sister was fucking with her either after she alienated herself from us. Journey walked over to me and gave me a hug and kiss, and the girl I was with sucked her teeth.

"Ugh, you need to get your company Jax. I am not the one." Journey said rolling her eyes and walking away.

"I better not ever hear or see you do any shit like that to my sister again."

"I'm sorry. I thought that was your baby mama."

"You won't be doing that shit to her either. Look, you and I are just fucking. Nothing more, nothing less. I brought you here, not as my girl, but as a friend that I'm going to fuck when we leave. You're welcome to leave anytime you want." She didn't say anything and sat there with an attitude.

"That's what the fuck I thought. Let me say goodbye to some people, and we can go." She asked for the keys to my car, and I asked that bitch was she crazy. She wasn't taking off in my shit. I went looking for Wolf and Passion to tell them I was leaving, but they were talking to the people that brought those nasty ass animals.

"My bad." I said when I bumped into someone. I was answering a text from the club manager, and I wasn't paying attention.

"It's ok." She said.

"What are you crying for?" I asked Venus when I saw her wiping her eyes.

"No reason. I'll see you later, Jax." I pushed her in one of the bathrooms and locked the door.

"Why are you crying?"

"No reason, Jax. Just go enjoy your company and leave me alone."

"That's what's wrong with you? You're mad I'm here with someone else?"

"Nope. I'm just going through the motions. This baby has me crying over everything." I lifted her chin with my two fingers.

"Don't lie to me Venus. You know I hate that shit."

"Ok fine. Yes, I'm crying because I see you with someone else, but it's my fault. I couldn't get passed my stubbornness, and I left you out to dry when you needed me. I needed you too, but I felt like I was betraying my brothers if I came back to you. I love you so much ,Jax, and yes it hurts when I see you with different women, but it's nothing I can do about it. I messed up and I have to deal with it. We hang with people in the same circles, so I'm sure this isn't the last time I'll see you with another woman. Are you happy now?" She asked and went to sink and turned the water on. She threw water on her face, and I handed her a paper towel.

"Thank you."

"Do you feel better?"

"Yes I do as a matter of fact."

"Good. Now you can sleep well knowing that you got that off your chest." I told her and opened the door. I know she was expecting me to say something else, but now it was me being stubborn and not allowing myself to go back to her. I watched her walk out, and her ass was bouncing in the dress she wore. I had to adjust my dick looking at her. I went to get the chick I came with and noticed Venus talking to some dude. Just that quick, she was smiling. I saw her pull her phone out and went walking to where she was.

"Get in the car and go the fuck home."

"Yo, Jax is this your girl? I didn't know."

"Nah, she ain't my girl, but she is off limits, and I want you to put the word out." Dude backed up with his hands up.

"You're a fucking asshole." She said and walked around to her car.

"I'll be that, but it won't be another motherfucker in that pussy, ever."

"Are you serious, Jax? This is the second woman I see you with, and I'm sure they're plenty more. I know you're sticking your dick that used to be mine in them, and you telling me I can't be with anyone else. You sound crazy."

"Yea, you sound crazy, Jax." The chick I brought came up behind me.

"Bitch, move the fuck on. This doesn't concern you."

"Why I got to be all that?"

"I'm telling you shorty, move the fuck on. Wait for me over there." She must've known I wasn't playing because she backed up.

"Jax, you let me know it was over. Leave me alone like I've left you alone."

"I am going to leave you alone, but like I said, ain't no other nigga feeling inside this pussy." I told her and grabbed it.

"Sssssss." She moaned out. I pushed her dress up a little and moved her panties to the side. I could feel her pearl getting hard as I played with it.

"Get off me." She pushed me away.

"Anytime you want some dick, you call me. That's the way it's going to be. Take it or leave it."

"I'll buy me a dildo and leave that nasty ass dick alone that you're fucking everyone with. I'd rather fuck with a toy than you." She said and got in her car. I knocked on the window and made her roll it down.

"WHAT?"

"Don't ever raise your voice at me, and I'll be over later."

"Don't bother motherfucker. I don't want you anywhere near me."

I was mad as fuck at her as she pulled away. I wasn't going to her house, but I wanted her to think that. She could say what she wanted, but I know she wanted me back just like I wanted her. That single life I was living right now was the shit and when I had enough I'll find my way back. I went and grabbed the chick up I came with and told her to get in the car. She rolled her eyes and slammed my door.

"Yo, suck my dick before I smack you for slamming my door." Most bitches would be mad when a nigga spoke to them like that, but not her. That shit turned her on. She sucked my shit real good when we pulled over in the park. I slipped a condom on and had her ride me. No pussy was as good as Venus's, but until I went back to her, this would have to do. After we both came, I dropped her off at home and went to my own place. I went inside and she was sitting on the couch waiting for me. I sat on the loveseat staring at her. I wanted her in the worst way, but I would never disrespect her like that.

"Jax, I don't want to fight with you every time I see you. Let's just be cordial with one another and co-parent when Jax Jr. comes."

"Fine. But I meant what I said when I told you no other nigga was ever feeling inside of you unless it's me."

"That's the shit I'm talking about, Jax. How am I supposed to be in another relationship with someone when you're talking like that?"

"You're not."

"I'm not what."

"You're not going to be in another relationship. You are my son's mother, and there is no more dating if it ain't with me."

"Ok, so you can't be with anyone else either then. If you want sex, it can only be with me."

"It doesn't work that way baby girl. Women are different, and you know that. What I look like having my son's mother parading around with another nigga?"

"You won't look like shit, because I wouldn't be with you so it shouldn't matter. I look like an idiot having my baby father flaunting around all these different women, and you don't care how that makes me look?" I thought about what she said. She was right; I didn't care how it looked. I didn't say anything and sat there staring at her. She got up and walked over to the door.

"Fuck you, Jax. Just stay away from me." She slammed the door behind her, and I stayed in the same position for about an hour, then I finally got up and took my ass to bed.

****

Over the next few days, I stayed home and had one of the bedrooms renovated into an office; I also had my man

68

cave built in the basement. I hadn't been back to the club since the shooting, because I didn't know who did it, and with me being there, I put innocent people in danger. I made sure the manager stayed in touch with me on a regular basis. I was putting up my new IMac in the office when my doorbell rang. I opened it, and it was Venus.

"Why you change the locks?" She asked pushing me to the side.

"So your crazy ass don't come in here one night and try to kill me." I shut the door and went in the kitchen to get something to drink. I lifted the top of the water and asked why she was there before I started drinking.

"You forgot we had a doctor's appointment today. I was calling your phone, but your stupid ass blocked me. You make me sick." I spit my water out and laughed at her.

"I'm sorry. I was renovating, and it slipped my mind. What did the doctor say?"

"You should've been there." She said and got up to go in the kitchen. She opened the fridge and took some grapes out and a bottle of Pepsi.

"Yo, take your ass home. Coming in here trying to eat and drink up all my shit."

"I wouldn't be if you went food shopping for me like you said you would."

"Oh shit, I'm sorry. I messed up twice Venus. Let me put something on, and we can go right now." I told her, and she waved me off. I put some sneakers on, grabbed my wallet, and came back down.

"Come on greedy." I yelled out, and she came out the bathroom.

I took her to Wal-Mart, Shoprite, and the farmers' market. She wasn't going to need any food for at least a month. I brought all the groceries up and helped her put them away. I glanced down at my phone, and it was a little after eight. I picked my keys up and yelled out to her that I was leaving. When she didn't answer, I went to check on her. She was stepping out the shower and wrapping the towel around her body.

"I'm leaving." She jumped and almost fell.

"You scared the shit out of me."

"My bad."

"What Jax?"

"I said I was leaving."

"Ok. Make sure the bottom lock is on, and I'll put the top one on when I'm done."

"I have the key; I can lock both of them."

"Ugh, I changed my locks a long time ago."

"Why did you do that?"

"So your ass didn't come try and kill me in my sleep." She said and started laughing. She was putting lotion on her body, and I stood there watching her like a creep, but she ignored me. It wasn't until she opened the towel, and I saw my son move in her stomach that it made her being pregnant more real.

"Did you see that?" I asked her.

"Jax, he is always moving like that." I found myself getting mad, because I was missing things like this. I got down on my knees in front of her and kissed her belly. She didn't say anything, and when I glanced up at her, she just smiled.

"He knows his father. He calmed down the minute you touched me."

"Good. Maybe you'll get a good night sleep.

"Yea, I hope so. Now that I have food in the house, I can fill my stomach up for both of us." She rubbed her stomach and started to put the nightgown over her head. I stood up and tossed it on the floor.

"You know I'm too big to be bending down to get that. Jax, you play too-" I cut her off by kissing her. I pushed her back on the bed and unbuttoned my jeans. I pulled them and my boxers down. I was in a rush to feel inside her, and I didn't want her to change her mind. Out tongues were still dancing together. I pushed my way in, and she was tight and wet as hell.

"Damn, baby. You still got the best pussy." I told her and continued stroking in and out of her.

"And you still have the best dick. I'm cumming for you."

"Then show me." She squirted out, and it was crazy looking at it go in different directions.

71

"I love you Venus."

"I love you too Jax. I know this doesn't mean we're together, but just make love to me like you used to." She said, and I gave her what she wanted.

"I just want to take things slow right now Venus, but I swear I won't sleep with anyone else." I told her after we finished.

"Jax, we're not together. I can't ask you to commit to that when you're single. I'm going to get dick from you when I want it and leave it at that. I love you with everything I have, but the minute I have this baby, if we're not together, there will be no more sex. You are Jax Jr.'s father, and no other man will be entertained by me as long as I'm pregnant."

"Venus, I will kill you if you sleep with someone else." She turned around to see if I was playing. I guess she knew I wasn't when she saw my face.

"Then, if that's the case, I'm whooping every bitch's ass you fuck with. And if you get her pregnant, I'm kicking it out her stomach."

"That's one thing you never have to worry about. No other woman is having my kids but you. I love you with everything I have, too Venus, but you fucked me up when I needed you and you left. You have to give me time to get over that. We should've been there for each other."

"Jax, I'm sorry. I really am, and I'll be here when you're ready to come back to me, but I meant what I said about beating up every girl you sleep with."

"And I meant what I said when I told you I would kill you if you slept with someone else." She rolled over and had her back to my chest. I rubbed her stomach until she went to sleep. I wasn't too far behind when sleep finally found me.

Journey

The day Colby took me to the hospital, they diagnosed me with Vertigo, and I had flu-like symptoms. Both of them together took a toll on my body, and the doctor said I should've come in when I first noticed that the dizzy spells didn't go away. I saw Colby's face when they were trying to get the needle in my arm to start an IV, and he was ready to fight everyone. After I was placed in a room and on antibiotics, a few hours later, I asked if they could they take me to see Colby.

My grandmother came and told me what happened in the waiting room with those two, and I wanted to make sure he was ok. Wolf refused to stay in the hospital, so when he came to, he signed himself out. Unfortunately, I got the shock of my life when I walked in my man's room, and his ex was standing there naked with a grin on her face. Colby looked as if he wanted to kill her, but I refused to hear anything he had to say. I was hurt, embarrassed, and I felt like a fool for taking him back.

When Wolf came over and talked to me about going to get my man back, I thought about what he said, and I wanted to, but what if he didn't want me back? I couldn't take the rejection so I left it alone.

He showed up at the doctor's appointment the next day, and once we found out that I was having a girl, he smiled and walked out. I couldn't tell you if he was happy or not. That entire day, I was depressed and stayed in my room all day. I was taking online classes now since I was pregnant, but the professor wanted me to come back after graduation and teach for him on certain days if I was up to it. I had two great offers now, but I wasn't sure which one I was going to take.

I went to Passion's son's birthday party, and it was a lot of fun. I couldn't wait until my daughter was having her first birthday. I was sitting in one of the chairs with some women talking about babies when I noticed Venus walk in. Then, some lady immediately went over to where Passion was and made her upset. Wolf handled that shit quick and came back like nothing happened. Venus stared at me a few times but didn't speak, and I damn sure wasn't speaking first. I reached out to her a few times after the hospital incident, and she avoided my calls. People can call me childish all they want, but I'm not going out of my way to speak, and I'm tired of hearing people say you should be the bigger person. Fuck that. Being the bigger person means not smacking the shit out of her for being a fake friend.

"Hey, let's go out to eat." My grandmother said, as she busted into my room as always.

"Where?"

"Who knows? I'm just tired of sitting in this house."

"Fine. I'll be down in a few minutes. Let me put some clothes on."

I got dressed and went downstairs only to find my Grams and her boyfriend waiting for me at the door. They were fondling one another, and the shit looked crazy. Neither one of them were old looking, but it just seemed crazy to see people their age still trying to get it in.

"Ugh, can we go now?" I said and opened the door. I walked out and started my truck.

"Child, don't be mad at me because I'm getting some dick and you're not." I rolled my eyes and drove us out to Chili's. I parked the car and went inside to tell the waitress we needed a table for three. There were a decent amount of people inside, and I prayed our food didn't take long. All I wanted to do was eat and go to sleep. A half hour later, we were having great conversation and eating our meal. I excused myself to use the bathroom.

"Journey." I heard a woman behind me as I washed my hands. I turned around, and it was some chick I had class with when I was working on my Bachelor's. She was always nice, and we had a few study groups together.

"Melissa."

"Yes. How are you?" She gave me a hug.

"I'm good. Just waiting to pop." I told her rubbing on my stomach.

"I see. Congratulations. Do you know what you're having?"

"A girl."

"That's great, Journey."

"Thanks. Do you have any kids?"

"Oh no. I'm just casually dating. This new guy I've been with the last two weeks may be the one though. He's handsome, charming, and his sex game is ridiculous." I covered my mouth to laugh at her.

"You are still a mess."

"What? His sex game is good. I mean, he claims he doesn't give oral sex, but with the way he puts it down, I don't need it."

"Yea, I miss those days with my ex, but you win some and you lose some."

"You're not with the baby's father?"

"No. It didn't work out, but we are going to be cordial for the baby. Well, let me get out of here before Grams comes in here yelling."

"Wait. Come meet my new friend and tell me what you think. You remember how we used to grade all the men in college. A one for gorilla ugly and a ten for super fine."

"I remember. Ok, let's go." She walked out in front of me and took me on the other side of the restaurant. Whoever she was sitting with had a hat on and his back was to us.

"Hey baby. Sorry it took me so long. I ran into one of my old college friends." I heard her say as I looked down at my ringing phone. It was Passion calling me. I hit decline and looked up to see her man, only to look into the face of Colby.

"Journey, this is my boyfriend, Colby. Colby, this is Journey." I didn't say anything, turned, then walked away.

"Journey wait." I heard him call out to me, but I didn't turn around. I told Grams I was ready to go and grabbed my things to leave. I tried to get out of there before the tears fell, but it was impossible being that more people were coming through the door. I had to say excuse me at least five times. Someone was probably having a party, because it was like twenty people. I got to my car and broke down. I don't know why, because I was the one who left him alone.

"I'm ready." Grams said, and the two of them got in the car.

"Is that Colby coming over here?" I turned my head, and it was him trying to run. I pulled out and sped off. I didn't have anything to say to him nor did I want him to see me crying. I made my choice, and now I have to deal with the consequences. When we got home, I grabbed a bag and told my grandmother I would be staying out. If I knew Colby, he'd try and stop by, and I needed to get myself together before I could deal with him. I checked in at the Marriott and made my way to the room. I opened the door and tossed my bag on the floor. I got on the bed, balled up in a fetal position, and cried. My daughter had me like a big ass baby. I cried so much I fell asleep. When I woke up, I had a ton of messages from Colby.

Colby: *Where are you?*

Colby: *I'm stopping by your house.*

Colby: *Your grandmother said you aren't home and told her you're staying out.*

Colby: *You better not be with a nigga*

Colby: *Journey just talk to me*

Colby: *I'm sorry*

The messages went on for about an hour. I dialed Passion's number back since she called me again. I had to make sure everything was ok with my brother. I was worried about her and Christian, too, but Wolf, Jax, and Grams is and will always be my main concern until my daughter gets here. Then, she'll be my top priority. She asked if I could stop by to help her with the books from the businesses. Wolf didn't want her working at Wal-Mart anymore so he set her up to manage the shop when Venus goes out on maternity leave; she would learn how to do the books. My brother was really changing for the better. I hung up with her and took a hot shower.

I brushed my teeth and washed my face that had dried up tears and boogers from the snot that came out when I was crying. I loved this hotel, because when you booked a suite, they gave you those thick complimentary robes. It felt so good on my skin.

Knock. Knock.

I wasn't expecting anyone and no one knew where I was. I opened the door thinking it was housekeeping and Colby pushed his way inside letting the door slam behind him. He pushed me against the wall and attacked my mouth with his then undid my robe. He removed it from my shoulders and began sucking on my neck and moved down to my breasts. I didn't want him to know how much he was turning me on and tried my hardest not to moan. It failed when his mouth latched onto my clit and I released one and all that I had in his mouth.

"Fuck. Fuck. Fuck." I moaned out after he gave me another one. My knees got so weak I had to hold onto the walls to stand up. He turned me around and had me arch my back a little as he continued devouring me from behind with no stopping in sight. I felt another one coming and this one was more powerful than before. My body was shaking as he inserted one finger in my pussy and the other in my ass.

"Let that pussy drip baby." He said, and I gave him what he wanted. I stayed against the wall with my face and chest feeling like they were glued to it from the amount of heat that radiated from my body. I heard him unzipping his jeans and the anticipation of feeling him inside me had my pussy jumping.

"Put it in. Oh God, I want to feel you right now." He was kissing on the back of my neck and back teasing me by placing the tip at my entrance then removing it. I moved my body closer to his to make him put his dick inside, but he would back up to be smart.

"Colby. I swear to God if you don't put it in-"

"What? You're going to do what Journey? Hold my pussy hostage like you've been doing. Huh? You like doing that shit." He entered me forcefully and didn't move.

"Ahhhhh Shittttttt." I came instantly. He grabbed my hair and pulled me up to him and my back was to his chest as he pumped in and out of me. His fingers were in my mouth, and his other hand was massaging my clit. The feeling he was giving me had me on an ultimate high. My eyes were rolling as another mega orgasm rocked my body.

"You missed your dick, didn't you?" He asked, and I couldn't speak because he now had me laid out on the bed with my legs spread apart hitting spots that were so deep that all I could do was try and breath.

"I'm done playing these games with you Journey. You're my fucking woman, and there ain't no breaking up. Do you fucking understand me?" Again I couldn't say shit. He started slowing down and waited for me to answer. "Do you hear me Journey?" I didn't answer again, and he started beating my pussy up.

"Yes Colby. Yes baby. No more breaking up. Oh shittttttttt." I screamed out and came everywhere.

"Get on top, and tell me it's you and me forever." I did like he asked and went up and down slowly. After a few minutes, I went up faster and came down harder. He was smacking my ass and fucking me from the bottom. I had to show him who had the best pussy since he was out there allowing other women to claim him.

82

"Colby, you don't really love this pussy." I said pretending like I was getting ready to stop.

"Don't play Journey. Fuck, just like that."

"I thought it was you and me forever." I said going in circles. "Why are you allowing other women to claim you?"

"Shittttt. I'm not baby. I don't know why she told you that."

"Is this my dick?"

"Fuck yea it is. You see where he's at." I went harder, and he sat up and held my body while he sucked on my chest. I could tell he was ready to cum by the way he started stiffening up.

"And where is that?"

"In the best pussy on Earth."

"Cum with me, Colby, and show me you mean it." He continued fucking me from the bottom as I went up and down harder and faster.

"Fuckkkkkk." We both screamed out at the same time and came together. We stayed in that position catching our breath. After a few minutes, I went to get up but he grabbed me back.

"Journey, I promise you there is no one else. I was sitting there alone, and she came over asking to join me."

"Did you sleep with her?"

"I have but not in the last couple days, and if I did today, I would've never disrespected you like that." He moved my head closer and forced his tongue in my mouth. I climbed back in the bed with him and allowed him to sex me down again.

"Come take a shower with me." He said removing the covers off my naked body.

"I'm tired. Just wash me up."

"No. I missed seeing that beautiful body and my daughter wants you to clean up too." He said making me smile. I followed him into the bathroom and allowed him to wash me up. He kneeled down and kissed my stomach over and over.

"Are you happy we're having a girl?" I asked him as we laid in the bed waiting on room service to bring up our food. We were both hungry from all the sex we had just had.

"I'm happy that you'll be the woman birthing all my kids whether it's a girl or boy. You know she'll be the first girl and is probably going to be spoiled worse than you?"

"I know. Passion has a boy, and we don't know what she's having this go round, but Wolf said he only shoots out boys. Jax is having a boy too, so this will be our princess." I said, and he kissed my forehead.

"I meant what I said, Journey, about no more breaking up. When I said I would never cheat on you again, I meant that. When you didn't believe me, I felt like there was no need for us to be together if you didn't trust that I was telling you the truth."

"I understand, and I promise to listen to you first."

"Good. Now go get the door because our food is here."

"Huh? I'm the one pregnant."

"And I'm the one that just gave you the best dick down you had in your life. I put work in." I sucked my teeth and put the robe on. I opened the door, and instead of it being food, it was some yellow roses. The guy asked me to sign for them, then I shut the door and went back in the room with Colby.

"Thank you baby. They're sweet." He gave me a crazy look as he stood up sliding on his pants.

"Where did you get those from?"

"The guy just brought them to the door." He snatched them out my hand and yanked the card out of it.

"Who knew you were here?" I saw him read the card.

"Huh?"

"WHO ELSE KNEW YOU WERE HERE?" He screamed making me jump.

"No one Colby."

"Get dressed."

"Why?"

"Don't ask questions just do it."

"Colby, I don't like the way you're talking to me."

"JUST DO IT, JOURNEY." He yelled and walked out with the flowers. I sat on the bed with an attitude. I wasn't doing shit until he asked me nicely. I heard him on the phone arguing with someone. I went to walk in there and the roses were on the table. I picked the card up and heard a ticking noise. I lifted them up and saw Colby running to me at full speed.

"NO JOURNEY." He yelled out, and I saw a flash in front of my eyes and felt my body hitting the floor.

Colby

I was sitting in Chili's waiting on this chick Melissa I was fucking with to come back from the bathroom when she asked me to meet her college friend. I had no idea why she wanted me to do that when the two of us were just friends. I didn't even bring her here. I was sitting by myself, and she came in with the two friends I fucked that night with her. She asked if I mind if she sat with me, and I shrugged my shoulders.

Melissa was a red bone that had a body for days and could possibly have been wifey material. The only thing was she wasn't Journey, and she was a hoe. Don't get me wrong, the pussy was definitely good, and so was that orgy we all had, but I wasn't giving up on Journey and I just yet. When I saw Journey and heard this dumb bitch say I was her man, I was pissed. Pissed because I was there alone and should've stayed that way, and two, the bitch was claiming me as her boyfriend. I cursed Melissa out, paid for my food, and ran after Journey. When she saw me, she pulled off.

I called and sent her text messages for over an hour, and when she didn't answer any of them, I had someone track her phone for me. She had booked a room at the Marriott, and her crazy ass used her real name. The minute she opened the door, I was all over her and she didn't put up a fight, which led me to believe she missed me just as much. I had her moaning, screaming and begging me to stop, but the roles were reversed when she got on top and gave me the ride of my life. I taught her well, and she surprised me every time with something new. The room service knocked on the door, and I was happy, because after all that sex, we both worked up an appetite. She walked in with some flowers thanking me like I was the one who sent them, so I snatched them out her hand and read the car.

"*Your brother took my son, and now I'm taking you.*"

That's what the card said, but I didn't know what he meant by taking her. I set them down on the table and called my father up. He was in a good mood and even asked me how my day went. I know it was him that sent the flowers, because that was his shitty ass handwriting. I swear he was really testing me.

"Hey son. It's a beautiful day today."

"Why did you send her those flowers?"

"Oh. I didn't know she told you." He said in a sarcastic tone.

"She didn't motherfucker! I'm here with her, and how did you know where she was?"

"Son, you know it's never too hard to find someone. However, she was definitely a hard one to get. I couldn't locate her for a long time until your ex saw her at the hotel."

"I'm going to kill that bitch."

"Now son, is that any way to talk about the woman that's going to comfort you while you're mourning your precious Journey?"

"What?" I saw Journey come out the room and pick the card up to the flowers.

"You heard me. Those flowers have a small device that will explode in about." I dropped the phone and tried to get to her before it went off. I could see Journey looking at me with fear on her face.

"NO JOURNEY." I screamed out as I watched her drop the flowers at the same time they blew up knocking her to the floor. I lifted her up and carried her to the couch. I picked the hotel phone up and told them I needed an ambulance right away.

"Journey baby, can you hear me?" I waited for a response and didn't get one. I checked over her, and that's when it hit me that she didn't get dressed like I told her too.

"Fuck. No. No. No." I yelled out when I saw blood coming from in between her legs. I heard banging on the door and then it opened. There were two police officers and a couple of EMT's.

"Sir what happened here?" The cops asked, and I tried to tell him, but I couldn't. My eyes remained on Journey and the blood that was on her legs. I watched the EMT's place her on the stretcher. I told them to cover her, because she only had a robe on and her body was showing. I grabbed my cell off the floor and followed behind them without answering the cops. I jumped in the back of the ambulance holding her hand and praying that God would let her make it out of this.

"How many months is she?"

"She will be seven in a week. Is she going to be ok? Is my daughter ok?"

"Sir, I don't know. Right now, her heart rate and pressure are low." My phone started ringing again, and it was my father.

"I see it worked."

"You better pray her and my daughter make it through this, because if not, there's nowhere you can hide." I said and hung the phone up. I jumped out when we got to the hospital and watched them rush her to the back again. I picked my phone up and called Venus. I needed her to give me Jax's number. I wasn't fucking with them like that, but he was the more level-headed one when it came to talking.

"Hey bro."

"Listen, something happened to Journey, and I need to get-"

"Hold on, Colby. I can't understand you. You sound like you're crying. Are you ok? Where are you?" I didn't realize I had tears coming down my face until she mentioned it. I saw the way the nurses and everyone else were staring at me and walked out.

"Venus something happened to Journey and the baby."

"WHAT?"

"You have to call her brothers."

"Jax is right here, hold on."

"What?" He said and I wanted to hang up but it was his sister.

"Get to the hospital." Was all I said and hung up. I didn't feel like arguing or explaining myself anymore. I sent Wesley a text and asked him to call Journey's grandmother and sent him her number. I was no good right now, and the smallest thing was going to make me kill a motherfucker. Twenty minutes later, Grams and her boyfriend, Wesley, Jax, Wolf, Passion, her son, and Venus walked in.

"What happened?" Wolf came straight to me. I guess he saw how upset I was and didn't talk any shit. Venus came and sat next to me, but I still didn't speak. I was trying my hardest to get myself together so I wouldn't break down again. I leaned back, blew out a breath, and wiped my face.

"It's ok, Colby. Just tell us when you're ready." I heard her grandmother say.

"FUCKKKKKKK!" I yelled out. I could see people staring. My leg was shaking as Venus rubbed my back.

"Ok, so we were at a room waiting for room service when someone knocked on the door. She went to get it and came back with roses that she thought I sent her. I snatched them away from her and read the card because they weren't from me. I asked her who knew she was there and she told me no one. Once I read the card, I knew who sent them. I was on the phone arguing with him. She came out the room and picked them and the card back up. Fuck, I should've thrown them away." I said trying to calm myself down.

"What happened to my sister?" Jax asked. I could see the scared look both of her brothers had on their faces. It wasn't the scared look of someone coming after them, but the look that they thought Journey was dead, and right now, I couldn't tell them that she wasn't.

"I yelled at her, and she dropped the flowers, but there was a small explosion." Her grandmother covered her mouth, and Wolf jumped up. I felt the tears coming down my face and didn't care who saw them.

"Her body hit the floor before I could get to her. I picked her up, and she had blood coming from her legs. I think she may have lost my daughter."

"WHAT?" Who did this?" Wolf had me jacked up by the shirt, and at this very moment I couldn't fight him off. I was slowly dying not knowing what was going on with Journey. Whatever he did to me didn't matter.

"Wolf get off of him." I heard her grandmother and his girlfriend yell. He let me go slowly and started tearing the hospital up. He was like a fucking maniac in there. He was tossing chairs out the window and even turned the vending machine over. I looked around for Jax, and he had the security guard held up at gunpoint telling him to take him to the back to check on his sister. My father was right. These niggas were losing their minds over her. A few minutes later, about ten cop cars showed up and arrested both of them. The entire scene was chaotic, and the only one to blame was my father, and he was going to get what was coming to him sooner than later. Not too long after they left, the doctor came out and we all stood up.

"Ms. Banks suffered really bad head trauma, and it caused a little swelling on the brain. Not enough that has us too concerned. She did require a few stitches in her head as well. She has a broken left arm and some pretty bad second-degree burns on her right side, but she's going to be just fine."

"How is my daughter?"

"Oh are you the father?"

"That's a dumb ass question don't you think?" I asked him and her grandmother smacked the back of my head.

"I'm sorry. We had to do an emergency C-section because the trauma to her body made her go into early labor."

"How is my daughter?" I asked him again. This time through gritted teeth because I felt like he was taking too long to answer.

"Actually, she's doing a lot better than expected." I let the breath go that I was holding in. To hear both of my girls were ok had me breathing a little better.

"Right now, she's in the NICU and will most likely be there for a few days. She was only four pounds but she is a screamer." He chuckled.

"When can I see them?"

"You can see Ms. Banks now, and then, they'll take you to your daughter."

"Why can't I see both of them at the same time?"

"Sir, like I stated before. Your daughter is in the NICU, because she was born very early. She has to stay there to be monitored closely. Her lungs aren't fully developed yet, and she will need to gain weight. I've already instructed the nurses to give you the bracelet so that you may come in and out the hospital along with her mom whenever you want to see her. I'm sorry that this happened to you, but she is in good hands right now… they both are. If you have any questions, please don't hesitate to call." I nodded my head.

"You guys can follow me upstairs to the floor we have her on, but dad, you will be the only one allowed in to see your daughter."

"You better take a ton of pictures of my great grandbaby." Grams said and pushed me in the room with Journey.

"Hey baby, how are you feeling?" I asked when she looked at us. She smiled.

"Give me a kiss first." She said, and I did what she asked. The crazy part is that she used her tongue and the shit was turning me on.

"Ugh, y'all act like we not standing here." Grams said.

"I'm sorry. That's my hero right there. If it wasn't for him being there with me, I don't know if I would be here with you. I'm sorry for not getting dressed when you told me too. And I'm sorry for picking those flowers back up." I sat on the bed next to her.

"Don't be. I'm just glad you're ok. You call me a hero, and I think that you're really one. The way you held our daughter in your stomach until you got to the hospital was nothing short of a miracle." I moved the hair out her face and kissed her again.

"Did you see her yet? The nurse told me she is beautiful."

"No, I'm going when I leave you. I'm sure she is just as gorgeous as her mother."

"Where are my brothers?" She tried to sit up and see if they were coming in. I was going to tell her in a nice way but Grams beat me to it.

"Those two motherfuckers cut a fool downstairs when they found out what happened to you. Wolf was acting just like his name, and Jax was trying to hold people hostage to get back there to you. The cops came and they got arrested. You know those niggas will go crazy if anything happened to you."

"Colby, I know I shouldn't be asking you this, but can you make sure that they get out." Her grandmother looked at me.

"Baby, I'm sure they're out already."

"Colby please. I can't have my brothers in jail." She started tearing up, and she knew I hated to see her cry.

"Ok baby. I promise I'll check on them."

"Can you call down there for me now."

"You know you owe me when you get better."

"Come here." I leaned down to her.

"I'm going to suck your dick so fucking good, you're going to be begging me to stop." My phone fell out my hand when she whispered that shit in my ear. I was fumbling trying to pick it back up.

"Damn boy, what did she say that got you nervous?" Grams' boyfriend said and they all laughed. I smiled and walked out the room to check on them. I called down there and they told me they were in a holding cell and that their bond was five thousand dollars each. I told them I would be down there in a few. I went back in the room and the nurse was in there. Journey told her I was the dad, and she gave me a bracelet and escorted me to the NICU floor. They had me put on some blue scrub thing with a shower cap looking hat and a mask. I felt like I was about to perform surgery. The woman walked me over to the room that had my daughter in it. She pointed to her crib, and I walked over there. She was tiny as hell. I wanted to hold her but they told me she had to stay in that incubator shit. I put my hands through the holes and she grabbed my finger. My daughter was already strong. She would be knocking bitches out in no time.

I stayed up there for about an hour talking to her, taking pictures, and listening to the nurses tell me how cute she was. I went back down to Journey's room, and everyone was still there. I took my phone out and showed them the photos. My girl was crying and Grams shed a few tears, but Venus was still off in the corner not saying a word. I had no idea those two still weren't speaking yet.

"Grams, can you call Drew and ask him to come keep an eye on her. I already told them in the NICU department that if anyone asks to tell them she lost the baby. I can't have anyone coming up to the hospital trying to do something to her." She nodded her head, then I grabbed Venus' hand and told Wesley to come with me to the jail.

"Why aren't you talking to Journey?" I asked her and she didn't respond. I glanced down at my phone and my father sent me a photo of the television screen that said a woman almost died from a small explosion in the hotel. I showed Wesley and he just shook his head. My father was going to get what he deserved and so was Willow for telling him where she was. I should've been killed her after that stunt she pulled in the hospital but left it alone because I was no longer with Journey but she fucked up.

"I don't know what to say."

"What the fuck you mean you don't know what to say? She just had your niece and almost died. You sat your ass in the corner not saying shit."

"I haven't spoken to her since the day we found out about Dice. She called me a few times but I didn't answer. Jax and I just started talking again from that, and I planned on speaking to her but then this happened, and I didn't want to bring it up."

"Make sure you take your ass up there when we leave. You were supposed to be her best friend Venus; that was foul as hell. You know she doesn't have any female friends but you, Passion and now her ghetto ass sister, Darlene."

"I know and I will." We pulled up at the station and got out.

Wolf

When Grams called me up and said we needed to get to the hospital because something had happened to my sister, I knew it had something to do with Colby's father. Passion got up and went to grab Christian out the room, and the entire ride over, I prayed that nothing happened to her, but with him, I didn't know. I stepped in the hospital at the same time as everyone else. When I saw Colby's face, I automatically thought the worst; especially how choked up he was and the fact that he couldn't get his words out. This nigga was crying real tears for my sister, and right then, if I didn't know before that he was in love with her, I knew now.

When I had him up by his shirt, and he didn't react, I knew he was hurting because he would've said or did something. I fucked that hospital up while Jax's crazy ass held a gun to the damn security guard demanding to get in the back. He knew that he couldn't have a firearm being a felon, so I made sure my grandmother told him that, if he didn't say anything, I would pay him.

"I see you two found out that your sister died or is just about dead." I heard his ass say. I smelled his nasty as cigar and turned around to see him standing there with Willow who looked pregnant.

"You better pray she's not dead, and bitch, what are you doing here?"

"I'm here with my baby daddy."

"Yuk. You fucked his old ass." Jax said shaking his head and laughing.

"Colby and Wolf were being stingy with their dick and I wanted a baby. I almost got it with Colby, but it didn't work out the way I wanted one so here I am about to be rich and a mama."

"You not only look stupid but you sound it. That man is going to kill your dumb ass right after you have it." She looked nervous when I said that, but he had a smirk on his face.

"No he's not. I'm going to have a few kids by him." I laughed at her. She was dumb as hell if she thought this man was keeping her around. I couldn't even talk to her dumb ass anymore.

"What the fuck you down here for? And how did you know we were here?" I asked and he blew smoke in the cell.

"I have my ways, and I came to offer you a deal."

"A deal." Jax said and stood up.

"What kind of a deal?" I looked at Jax like he was crazy.

"See I like you. You're about the business while he is about the kill."

"What's the deal?"

"If you kill both of my sons, I promise to leave your sister alone."

"Hold up. You want us to kill your kids? What type of shit are you on?" I said walking back over to where he stood.

"They're not strong enough for me. Colby allowed pussy to take him off his grind, and Wesley only does what Colby says. Dice was the realest one out of them, and well, you took him away from me."

"Yo, you're bugging."

"Wait a minute, Wolf. I don't want anything else happening to Journey if she makes it. Let's think about it. Listen, we'll talk it over and get in touch with you." Jax said and gave him the dirtiest look. The two of them walked out, and Jax sat back down on the bench.

"You know Journey will never forgive you if anything happens to him." I said and laid my head back on the wall.

"I know. That's why we have to plan the shit perfectly. If he thinks Colby and Wesley are dead, he will stop gunning for her and let his guard down." I thought about what he said, and it made sense to me, but I wasn't so sure it would make sense to my sister. She doesn't handle death well at all since my parents. I don't know how she will be able to pull off faking his death.

"Jax, I think if this is what we're going to do, you should be the one to ask her. The two of you have a better relationship."

"Nigga, shut up. She talks to both of us the same. Your punk ass don't want to see her cry when you tell her she has to fake his death. You hate to see her cry and start getting all mushy and shit."

"Fuck you, Jax. Let's see who gets mushy when Venus drops that baby."

"Oh, I'm sure I'll shed a tear. A woman pushing a baby out is a miracle, and I can't wait to watch."

"Man, I hope Journey didn't lose Armonie." I said to him. That was the name she picked out for her.

"She didn't." We heard Colby say as he stood there on the other side of the bars.

"Matter of fact, the both of them are awake and doing fine."

"She had her." Jax was excited as hell.

"Yea, but she has to stay in the NICU until her lungs develop and she gains more weight. Do you want to see her?" He took his phone out, and we both looked at the photos.

"Why does she have all those wires on her? Is she hurting? I mean, that's too much on her." I said handing him back the phone.

"No, she's good. One is the IV, and the other is oxygen. The one with the red light on her toe is to make sure she's breathing. Trust me, I asked all those questions when I was in there." We both nodded and stood there waiting to see who would speak first.

"Soooo, Journey asked me to come down here and get you guys out. I'm not going to lie and say I wanted to, but she made me an offer I can't refuse." He stood there grinning.

"Yo, I know y'all just had a baby but spare me."

"Don't be like that, Jax. I gave you an offer this morning that you couldn't refuse."

"Really, Venus?" Colby said as she walked back there.

"What? Shit we all fucking; it ain't no secret. That's exactly what I'm going to do to my jail bird when he gets released." Colby was aggravated, and Jax put his head down laughing.

"Anyway. We don't have to like each other, but I love your sister, and she's going to be my wife. We can either squash this beef and be cool like we used to be or just don't say shit to one another. It doesn't matter to me, because as long as I got my girl and my daughter, I'm good." He said and we couldn't do shit but respect that.

"I know you love her, but the next time you pull a gun out on her for leaving you, it won't be no talking." I said, meaning every word. He nodded his head letting me know he understood.

"Ok you two. Your bail has been posted. Expect the court date in the mail, and if you don't show up, a warrant will be issued for your arrest." The officer said opening the cell.

"Yea. Yea."

"Oh my goodness. I was so worried baby." Passion came up to me when I walked out the station. She had

Christian with her, and he was trying to get out of her arms to get to me. I took him from her and kissed his cheek.

"Where were you?"

"I was at the hospital. Grams said I can't bring him in the jail, so when Colby said he was coming, I waited in the car. Haven, you have to see your niece. She is so pretty. I can't wait to hold her."

"I saw her on his phone and don't think I didn't hear you say my real name."

"But I love that name, and you let me say it when you're making love to me."

"Oh shit. That nigga Wolf knows how to make love?" Jax said, and everyone looked at me.

"Yes he does, and he does it very well. Ain't that right baby?" She pulled me down to her level and planted a kiss on my lips.

"Whatever. I'll meet you at the hospital." I told him and got in the truck.

"Passion don't be telling people what I do."

"I didn't know I was loud and don't be ashamed that the almighty Wolf knows how to make love to a woman. I love the way you make me feel and how gentle you are around us, but I understand you want to uphold that image so I won't mention it again."

"Thank you, and I will always be gentle to you. You have my heart now, and I won't do anything to make you break it by being mean or rough with you. I know a man can break a woman down mentally and physically, and I never want to do that to you. You are my queen and you deserve the same respect I give my mom, even though she's no longer here, my Grams and my sister. Well, I don't know now that she had my niece; I may have to put all of you on the back burner."

"I have no problem with that. As long as she is the only female that comes before me, unless we have a daughter, then she will be too."

"Yup. Now let's go see my sister so I can get home and put a shift in your uterus."

"You make me sick."

"But you love it."

"You're right I do." She leaned over and kissed me.

*****

I walked into my sister's room, and she looked like shit, but I wouldn't tell her that. She had a bandage on her head, a sling on her left arm, and some bandages going down her right arm. There wasn't anything wrong with her face, but Colby already told me that the burns went down the entire side of her right body. I was happy that I couldn't see it, because it would just make me angrier than I already was.

She tried to sit up, but I could see that she was in pain, so I sat next to her on one side of the bed, and Jax sat on the other side but at the end. It seemed like everyone disappeared out of the room. I pushed her hair back some, and she laid her head on my shoulder and placed her feet on Jax's lap. We asked her what happened, and she told us the exact story that Colby said. It wasn't that we didn't believe him, but sometimes you want to hear it again to make sure you heard it correctly. She cried as she told us she thought she was going to die, and that she wasn't sure if the baby made it.

"Did you two see her yet?" She asked wiping her tears.

"Your boyfriend showed her to us at the jail. She looks like you and mom." Jax said.

"I know right. I haven't been able to go up there yet. Where is Colby?"

"That nigga went straight up there to check on her again." I told her, and she started laughing.

"Do you know who sent me those flowers?" Both of us turned our heads. I tried to change the subject, but she wasn't trying to hear it. "Don't do that. Who sent them?"

"His father. He wants you dead, because he thinks it will hurt us more if he gets you and not Wolf." Jax told her. I got up to use the bathroom.

"I don't understand why he's doing this. He took two people away from us, and he's still trying to take more. Why won't he leave us alone?" She was crying on Jax's shoulder, who was now in the bed with her when I came out the bathroom.

"Don't worry, we have a plan? And no we're not going to tell you right now so don't ask. All I want you to do is focus on getting better for my niece when it's time for her to go home." She nodded her head and stayed under Jax. I pulled

106

the chair up to the bed and leaned backwards on it with my feet on the radiator. We used to do this when I was young and she would run her hand over my head like she was doing now. We sat there for a while when I heard the door open.

"Well damn; I guess there's no love for me." Colby said when he walked in.

"Always, baby, but you know how I am when it comes to them."

"I know. I just wanted to tell you I love you, and I'll see you tomorrow."

"You're not staying."

"You got your brothers here, and I don't want to take time away from them."

"Nah, it's all good. Venus ain't letting my ass stay out." Jax said standing up.

"And Passion just text me that dinner was ready if you know what I mean."

"Yuk, Wolf." She said and sucked her teeth.

"It's better than this nigga coming to the jail saying you gave him an offer he couldn't refuse in order for him to come down there." She looked at him.

"COLBY?!" She started laughing.

"What? You did."

"It's ok sis. We know he knocking it down. Grams tells all your business." Jax said, and she turned beet red.

"That's it. Her ass has to go." Everybody started laughing.

"Wolf and Jax." Both of us turned around when she called us.

"Yea."

"Thank you for not killing Colby, and Colby, I appreciate you swallowing your pride and getting my brothers out. I love all of you, and I want, no I need all of you in my life. Please and I'm begging all three of you, please just try to get along for Armonie and me. I don't want her or my future nieces and nephews growing up watching you go to war with each other." She had tears running down her face, and Colby went and sat next to her.

"Stop crying, Journey. You know I hate to see you hurting."

"I know but-"

"Journey, we cool." Jax told her and kissed her forehead.

"Don't lie to me because I'm crying."

"He's not babe. We squashed it at the jail for you. I'd rather make peace with them if it's the only way I can keep you in my life." He told her. This nigga was a straight sucka for my sister.

"I love you, Colby." She wrapped her hand around his neck and kissed him.

"Ugh ok. We'll see you tomorrow sis. All this lovey dovey shit you two do is too much." I told her and kissed her cheek. Jax gave Colby a look that told him to come outside.

"I'll be right outside Journey."

"I love you sis."

"I love you, too, Wolf."

"JAX." She yelled out, and he came back in the room.

"Yea."

"I love you."

"I love you, too, sis. Stop being a brat and get some rest."

"I will. Send my man back in when you're finished with him."

"Bye Journey." I told her and shut the door. I loved my sister to death, but she was acting like a spoiled brat, and I was happy as hell someone else had to deal with her now.

Jax

I walked out my sister's hospital room with every intent to leave, but I couldn't without figuring out what the plan was. This man was causing too much drama in our lives when he was the one who started it from the beginning. I waited for Wolf to close the door before I spoke, because I didn't want her to hear anything. We walked down the hall and found a spot where no one could hear us. Everything that needed to be said would have to be kept between the three of us if we didn't want any mistakes.

Colby was glancing down at his phone and lifted his phone up to show us what his father sent him. It was a photo of yellow flowers asking which funeral home he needed to send them to. I know parents don't get along with their kids, but this was dysfunctional as hell.

"What's up?"

"Your pops came down to the jail and offered us a deal."

"A deal. What kind of deal?"

"The deal was to kill you and Wesley in order for him to leave Journey alone."

"WHAT?" This nigga was thirty-eight hot when I told him that. People and some of the nurses started staring in our direction.

"Look, I know you're mad, but the only way we can get rid of him is to fake your death and make him let his guard down."

"HELL NO! There's no way in hell I'm leaving Journey and my daughter." He started pacing back and forth.

"I'm just going to go over there and kill him myself."

"Whoa." Wolf said and stood in front of him.

"If you go over there, you may as well say goodbye to Armonie and Journey, because you'll be walking into a trap. You think he's not waiting for you? The reason we had to talk to you here is because I'm sure he will have someone watching. Unless you have a better idea, this is the only way."

He went and sat on one of the chairs in the waiting area. I could see stress written all over his face. I would be doing the same thing if I were in the position he was. He took about five minutes to get himself together before he came back to us.

"Fine ,but you have to let me propose to her first." Wolf and I stared at him.

"You want to marry my sister?" I stood there with my arms folded, and Wolf did the same thing.

"Without a doubt. If I could marry her right now, I would, but she always spoke of a big wedding and I won't take her dream from her. But I have to propose first."

"Listen, if it makes you feel any better, you don't have to leave. You can stay in the house with her, but you'll be confined to just there. You won't be able to leave the house or even sit outside in the back yard. You have to remain out of sight in order for it to work." I told him and he nodded his head.

"Why didn't you say that in the beginning? I will never have a problem laying up under her."

"Alright, that's too much." I told him and he laughed.

"Ok then; it's settled. When do you plan on proposing?"

"The doctors said she could leave in a few days. I want to have a small welcome home party for her, and I'll do it there."

"Ok cool. I'll let Grams know. Trust me, she'll be excited. All we ever wanted was for Journey to be happy, and if that's what you want to do for her then we're all for it."

"We see how much you two love each other." Wolf said.

"Yea that's my heart right there. Well, now her and Armonie are."

****

When I left the hospital, I was going straight to Venus' house. I didn't want to rush out in the morning before I went back to the hospital so I stopped by my house to grab some clothes. I locked the door up and looked down at my phone that notified me I had a message. It was Venus' greedy ass asking for some Popeye's, so I went there and couldn't believe my eyes. I got out the car and went inside to see if I could hear anything since no one was in there. There was a partition up with all that funny looking glass so they couldn't tell I was standing there.

"Wesley, if you don't do it, I am going to disown you."
I heard his father say.

"Pops, you already got the sister, why can't you leave
well enough alone?"

"Because I want your brother dead. He should've went
ahead and killed her like I told him to."

"Pops, he loves that chick. How would you be feeling
right now if your dad did some shit like that to you. She may
have lost the baby, your grandchild and all you're focused on
is killing your own son. You can be mad all you want, but I'm
not killing him."

"Wesley, you're going to do what the fuck I say or I
promise I'll tell him the truth about you."

"You think I give a fuck if you tell him I fucked his ex.
Do you honestly think he'll care?"

"He will when he finds out you were fucking Willow at
the same time he was and got her pregnant. What you think
he'll say when he knows the two of you have a three-year-old
that your aunt is raising as her own."

"Pops come on."

"You know he was in love with Willow at that time.
Remember how messed up he was when he found out she
cheated on him. It's going to be even harder to hear you were
the one."

"Welcome to Popeye's, can I take your order?" The
cashier said, and I moved in closer to tell her what I wanted. I
was trying to hurry up so I could listen some more. By the

time I paid for my food and went back over there, they were gone. They must've gone out the side door, because they didn't walk by me at all. I called Wolf up and told him what I heard and he found the shit funny. I guess I did too, but I would be highly upset if my brother did some shit like that to me knowing I was in love with the chick.

"You ain't shit bro."

"What? The bitch is a ho, and Colby should be happy he found out before it was too late. Yea, it's fucked up his brother fell victim to her but the bitch don't even have grade A pussy, and she don't swallow. I only stayed fucking her because she could suck dick and was convenient as hell."

"Ok, so the father had us trying to kill both of them while he has the brother on the same mission. We are going to have to let Colby know and speed up the process. If anything happens to that nigga, and Journey knows we had an idea, she will never speak to us again."

"I know. Let me go in here before Passion comes looking for me. Why didn't you tell me pregnancy makes these chicks want to fuck a lot?"

"Some things you have to learn on your own." I laughed and hung up. I pulled in front of Venus' house and my phone was going off again. It was the chick I had at the birthday party with me. I opened up the phone because it was a text message and there were a few shots of her pussy with a message asking me to come over. As bad as I wanted to, I couldn't. I promised Venus we would take it slow and that I wouldn't sleep around. She opened the door and had on nothing but her towel.

"Yo, don't answer the door like that again."

"Whatever. Just give me my food. I'm hungry." She snatched the bag out my hand and went in the kitchen. I watched her ass peeking from under that towel and became aroused instantly. I was trying not to have as much sex with her because she was bigger and we both enjoyed rough sex, but that shit flew right out the window when I got out the shower.

"Ugh, what's this?" I asked stepping into her personal space as she laid on the bed with her legs open.

"Nothing, I thought I'd take some pussy shots and send them to your phone." She held my phone in the air and then tossed it at the wall.

"Girl, don't nobody want her. If you would've looked at the message I sent her, you would've saw I texted her that I didn't want to fuck her anymore, and that I was back with my girl."

"Oh, I saw it. I also saw her say she didn't care. You know I'm fucking her up on sight right?'

"Just shut up and give me some of my pussy." I told her and made love to her. I wanted rough sex, but like I said, right now, with her being eight months, I couldn't risk it, but she was going to regret running her mouth once she dropped my son. I was going to make sure she couldn't walk for a week.

Over the next few days, I had been back and forth up to the hospital visiting my sister. No one was allowed to see my niece yet, because she was still in the NICU, but between her and Colby, I don't know who had more photos. That nigga was there every day and only went home when Wolf or I came. I think he was scared to leave her alone, and I didn't blame him. I wasn't feeling her being there alone either. They were releasing her from the hospital in a few days, and she cried like a baby, because she didn't want to leave Armonie. Little did she know, Colby had one of the extra rooms at the house set up like the NICU room? He even had one of those incubator cribs there and hired some nurses to come by. Wolf and I paid a lot of money to have one of the ambulances bring Armonie when it was time to go.

*****

"What's up Penny?" I said when she stepped out her car in front of the club.

"Do you know your brother shot me the day you came home?" I gave her a dirty look. When someone steps to you like that, most likely it's a fucking set up.

"Bitch, my brother didn't shoot your stupid ass. It was probably one of those many niggas or their bitches you sleep with."

"Jax, all I wanted to do was get back together with you. Yea, I may have told that chick we slept together, but your brother didn't have to shoot me." There she goes again saying that. I stepped around her and opened the door with her following me still talking shit.

"Stop saying he shot you. I was there, and you got in your own car and drove home. Why do you keep saying that dumb shit?"

"So you don't care that Wolf almost killed me?"

"Penny, I suggest you take your lying ass the fuck out of here. I don't know what you're trying to do, but you lying on my brother is not going to fly with me."

"What? You're going to kill me too?" She said stepping closer to me. *Yea, it was definitely a setup.*

"Listen, Penny. I know the real reason you're here is because you miss this big dick fucking up your insides." She folded her arms and rolled her eyes. "I'm sorry to be the one to tell you, but my girl fucks the shit out of me so good I don't need to look elsewhere. As far as my brother goes, stop spreading that damn lie that he shot you, because we both know he wouldn't raise his hand or a gun to a woman. Now, get the fuck out of my club, and I don't want to see you in here again." She looked at me and I gave her a wink and a smirk. I wanted her to know I knew what she was up to without saying it.

"Fuck you, Jax." She stormed out and almost fell.

"That's what you want, but it's not happening bitch." I yelled out behind her and closed the door. It was too early for that shit. There were a few people at the club when she did that dumb shit, but no one I was too worried about. I opened my office door and sat down at my desk playing with the new phone I got since Venus' crazy ass broke the other one. I went ahead and got a new number too since we were basically back together and no women needed it. I got a text message from Venus, and she sent me some naked pictures. I know she was being smart, but I appreciated the hell out of them.

"You playing games this evening young lady."

"What? I just want to make sure my man knows what he has at home." Venus said seductively into the phone.

"I definitely do, and you know no one will make me mess that up." She and I had spoken for a few more minutes before another problem walked through my door. I hung the phone up and adjusted my pants, because this bitch was doing the most. By the time she reached my desk, she was already naked and trying to undo my jeans.

"Come on, Jax. I need it." The chick from the party moaned in my ear. She had me ready to fuck the hell out of her, but I couldn't do that to Venus.

"Nah. I'm back with my girl. My dick is no longer for rent."

"Got damn you, Jax. You said you were going to be single for a long time and you weren't looking for a woman."

"I wasn't. Here, put your clothes on." I handed her things to her and stood there waiting for her to get dressed. When she did, she stood in front of me.

Tina J.

"I'm going to miss this dick, and I know you're going to miss the way I suck you off." She said and grabbed it on the way out. I shut the door and locked it.

Whew! That was close.

Venus

Jax left the house this morning looking good as hell. I wanted to try and make him stay home, but I knew he had to handle his business at the club. I did however send him a text with quite a few pictures that made him call me right up. You see. Jax and I are like horny dogs when it comes to sex. We'll fuck anywhere, anytime and don't care what anyone thinks. The only problem is, while I enjoy the way he makes love to me, I love the rough sex, and he told me no more until after we have the baby.

Today I was going to the hospital to visit Journey. My brother Colby let me have it the day she gave birth and the following days for not going to see her. She didn't have a lot of friends, and he was right by calling me foul for not answering her calls. It wasn't that I didn't want to talk to her; it was just a lot going on between our families, and I didn't know how to deal with it. I'm sure they were going through some things too, and we could've gotten through it together, but I was being childish. I parked in the parking lot and got my visitor's pass from the front desk. When I got off on her floor, I saw Colby coming out the room.

"Hey sis." He gave me a hug and asked me what I was doing up there.

"I came to apologize."

"Took your ass long enough."

"Whatever. Where are you going?"

"Upstairs to see my daughter. You know I don't leave this hospital unless one of her brothers are here." He kissed my cheek and left me standing there. The closer I got to the door, I could hear voices. I walked in, and Passion stood up to give me a hug, then I noticed her ghetto ass sister. I waved to her and went to the bed where Journey was.

She looked much better than when she was first admitted. The bandage was off her head, and she wasn't wearing any on her arms anymore, but you could see the burn marks the explosion left on her. She was up and dressed in a pair of leggings and a t-shirt.

"I'm sorry, Journey. I should've been there for you. I just didn't know how and I missed so much time with you and Jax being childish." I said and kept going until she told me to be quiet.

"What kind of shit is that? If she was my friend, I would smack the shit out of her for taking so damn long to apologize." Darlene said staring at me.

"This doesn't have anything to do with you Darlene." Passion told her.

"No, she's right Passion. I shouldn't have taken this long to apologize." I rolled my eyes at Darlene.

"Journey, my brother took your parents away and your brother took someone away from me. I know that you didn't know what was going on, hell none of us did except my father. I thought that, if I stayed friends with you and continued seeing Jax that I was betraying my family. You may not understand that, because you and my brother stayed together, and I admire the shit out of yall for that. The longer you two were together after everything came out, it showed me that what happened in the past should stay there. We all lost someone, and I missed the hell out of you and Jax." I felt the tears coming down my face. Journey stood up slowly and held onto the rail of the bed.

"You're right, Venus. You should've never been that childish, and I would most likely be pissed if I didn't have your brother there to lean on. He was my rock along with my brothers, Passion and even Darlene." Darlene gave me a fake smile and stuck her middle finger up at me.

"There were so many times that I wished you were there for me to talk to, but you just left me hanging. I don't know if we could still be friends, Venus. I would never want you to do that to me again."

"Stop giving her a hard time, Journey. You already said you forgave her." Jax said walking in the room.

"Dammit, Jax, why couldn't you just go along with it?"

"Look how sad you have my girl looking."

"Serves her ass right for leaving me hanging. And she needed to hear how I felt before she knew I forgave her." She put her arms out and gave me a hug. I had to be gentle with her, because Jax was about to fuck me up when she winced over in pain.

"So what's up Jax? We still hooking up later or what?" Darlene said and blew him a kiss.

"Bitch, I know you didn't just try and hit on my man."

"Hmph. It seems like he needs a woman who ain't childish."

"Darlene, beat it. You know damn well I turned that same ghetto ass proposition down a thousand times already. I know you want to see how big my dick is and take a ride on it, but my girl owns this, so you'll have to continue fantasizing about it." I busted out laughing, because all she could do was roll her eyes.

"Whatever. Nigga I don't want you anyway. Now your other brother Drew. He can get it quick, fast, and in a hurry." No sooner than she said that did Drew walk in; he looked at her and rolled his eyes.

"Why the fuck is she here?" He went and sat next to Journey.

"Don't be like that Drew? You know you want this again."

"AGAIN?!" We all shouted.

"Man, that's why I can't fuck with you. You may have some good pussy, but you talk too much. I told you we could hook up if you weren't so fucking ghetto."

"Ok. Damn, I told you I was trying to calm down."

"You better. Now take that ass home and wait for me." When she got up and did what he said, we all looked over at him. He was eating a hot dog looking up at the television.

"Really, Drew?" Journey asked him.

"I'm sorry sis." He stood up and placed a kiss on her forehead.

"I'm over all these different men kissing my future wife." Colby said coming in the room.

"Don't be jealous, baby. They don't get any of what you get."

"Mmmm." He moaned out after he pulled back from kissing her.

"Yoooo. That's still my sister. You can just peck her in front of us." Jax was mad as hell that they were tonguing each other down. Everyone started laughing. We were sitting at the hospital for about two hours having a good time. Wolf came up with Christian, and Passion's entire face lit up. She was really changing him for the better, and I could see how much he loved her.

"Yo Venus, did you just pee on me?" Jax asked me, because I was sitting on his lap. I looked down at his jeans and they were wet.

"No asshole. My water just broke. I tried to stand up, but you wouldn't let me. Come on so I can deliver your son." I said and stood up. I was happy the contractions didn't kick in right away; otherwise, me walking to the nurses' station wouldn't be happening.

"Are you excited?" I asked Jax while I was being pushed to the elevator. They were taking me to the Labor and Delivery floor.

"Yup. And you know I'm watching your pussy open up."

"JAX BANKS!"

"What? You're always saying my dick too big. Once you push my son out, there're no more excuses. The nurse started snickering.

"I fucking hate you."

"No you don't." He leaned down and kissed my lips.

Twelve hours later, I pushed out my eight pound, seven-ounce son, and he resembled the shit out of Armonie. I know they were first cousins, but damn they have some strong ass genes. It looks like I only carried him, because he didn't look anything like my side of the family. Jax thought that shit was funny, but I didn't. He and Wolf had jokes for days. Journey came in with my brother and started crying when she saw him.

"How do both of our kids look like mommy?" She said and the room seemed to get a little gloomy.

"That means your baby is going to look like daddy." She said to Wolf, and he sucked his teeth.

"I'm going to keep getting her ass pregnant until we have one that looks like her too then." Passion rolled her eyes when he said that.

"Don't roll your eyes. You wanted this. My dick and me. Therefore, you're stuck with me forever. That pussy ain't birthing no kids unless they come from me."

"Wolf, do you always have to be so vulgar?"

"Ugh, I'm not vulgar when I'm deep in those guts am I?" He said wrapping her up in his arms.

"I'm sorry guys. I thought we were making progress, but I have to start over."

"What does that mean?" Wolf said, and we sat there waiting to see what she was talking about.

"That means no pussy until you can be civilized."

"Yea ok. Try it and see what happens." Those two went back and forth for a few minutes before Journey told them she was leaving if they didn't stop.

"Well, I get discharged in two days, and I'm probably not going to see you, because I'll be up here every day until my daughter gets released." Journey said, and we all looked at Colby. We knew he had the room set up for Armonie, but I guess he didn't tell her.

A few hours later, everyone left, and I was happy because I was tired, and Jax Jr was hungry. It was crazy seeing a small replica of his father lying next to me. He opened his eyes a few times, and of course, they were gray like Jax's. He was so happy to finally be a father he didn't want to leave. I asked him to go and get the bag I packed. It had my clothes in it and the outfit I wanted him to take pictures in.

I was burping my son when she walked her ugly ass in my room with a smirk on her face. I knew who she was because she had that same short hairstyle from the BBQ. She pulled a chair up and sat down on the side of my bed. I didn't say anything and waited for her to speak. At first, she just stared at me, I guess, trying to see what my son looked like.

"Hmmm, I guess that is Jax's baby." She said and leaned back in the chair.

"Why wouldn't it be, and what are you doing here?"

"I know you were still fucking your ex before he came home, and when Jax finds out, I'm sure he won't be too happy to hear about it. See, I've known him since we were teenagers, and he doesn't take it well when he finds out someone lied or tried to play him."

"What do you want Penny? And as far as my ex, I stopped sleeping with him months before Jax came home." I wasn't even going to entertain her bullshit. So what if I was still messing with my ex? Jax was in jail fucking her. We both ended what we had with them when we made it official.

"I want that nigga Wolf to go to jail for shooting me."

"Wolf shot you." I acted surprised. Jax already came home and told me how she came to the club trying to get him to confess to it. I buzzed the nurses' station and asked her to take Jax Jr. back to the nursery. I felt like shit was about to go left and needed him out the room. I picked my phone up and texted Jax that he better get back up here before I catch a case.

"Bitch, don't play games with me. You know he did."

"Penny. I don't know what happened. You saw me leave when you came to the house and said that bullshit." She didn't say a word. It was like she couldn't think of anything to say.

"Penny, I don't know what you got going on in your life nor do I care. I do suggest you stop whatever infatuation you have with the Banks family. You're digging yourself a hole that you may not be able to get out of."

"Is that a threat?"

"What? Why would I threaten you? You didn't do anything to me. I think it's time for you to leave."

"I don't have to go anywhere." I stood up, and the pain wasn't as bad where I couldn't walk but it was hurting. I grabbed her by the shirt and started guiding her towards the door. She turned around and caught me on the side of my face, and after that, all I saw was red. I tossed her ass across the room and started punching her over and over. When I got tired, I kicked her in the ribs a few times until I was being lifted into the air. Jax pointed for me to go sit on the bed and lifted her dumb ass up out the corner.

"What's wrong with you? Why are you even here?"

"Jax, why aren't you saying anything to her for hitting me." Penny asked him and he laughed at her.

"Bitch, are you crazy? You come in my girl's room after she just gave birth to my son talking shit, and you expect me to say something to her for beating your ass. You're a lot more stupid than you look. Get the fuck out of here." He pushed her dumb ass out the room.

"I'm going to get you and your brother Jax. You just wait." She screamed from the door. He walked over to me and examined my body. I felt some blood gushing out on the pad and asked him to help me to the bathroom. He assisted me in the shower where I gave him head since we couldn't fuck yet. I told you we were freaks when it came to each other. I finished my shower and put some clothes on to feel a little more comfortable. He went to the nursery and brought Jax back in and laid him on his chest. I already knew he was going to spoil the shit out of him so I may as well get ready for it.

"Venus, can you give me another kid in about a year?"

"Huh?"

"I'm going to nut all up in that pussy after six weeks. I just want you to know that in another year you'll be in this same position. And your ass better not get on fucking birth control."

"Jax why can't we wait for two years?"

"Because we'll probably be walking down the aisle by then." I lifted my head up from the magazine I was reading. He was putting Jax Jr. in his crib and sat on the edge of the bed with my hand in his.

"I love you, Venus. You held me down for the latter part of my bid, and you handled all my needs. I'm not going to give you a long speech, because I know you're waiting for me to ask you, and that's not what I'm doing, so relax."

"You play too much." I pushed him in the chest.

"I'm just playing, baby. Will you marry me?" He took a black box out his pocket, and there was a huge, emerald green diamond ring.

"You remembered." I had tears coming down my face.

"I did." I always told him that my mom had a green emerald ring that her mother gave her the day she married my father, but he threw it out when she left him. I told him I wanted an emerald, princess-cut diamond just like it, and that's what he was placing on my finger.

"Um, do you think I could get some more of that bomb ass head you just gave me in the bathroom?"

"Jax."

"I'm just fucking with you. When you stop bleeding, I'm going to fuck the shit out of you, you're going to beg me to stop."

"I don't expect anything different from you. I love you Jax."

"I love you too. Now move over so I can squeeze in this bed with my family." He took our son back out and put him on his chest. I picked up my cell and flashed my finger in the front before I took a photo and sent it to everyone. I was happy as hell.

Journey

Today was the day I was leaving the hospital without my daughter, and I wasn't happy at all. I cried up until Colby pulled the car to the front entrance. He came around to open the door and helped me get in. I put my seatbelt on and waited for him to climb back in. I stared at him as he drove, and I must admit, he was not only handsome, but everything I wanted in a man. Don't get me wrong; we had a rough start by all means, but we managed to stay together through it all. My brother Wolf sent a text to my phone asking where we were. He said my grandmother was waiting to see me. She had the flu, and the last time I saw her was when Armonie was born.

We pulled up to the house, and I saw everyone's car there. I was a little shocked being that they all claimed they had something to do. I opened the car door and Colby grabbed my things out of the back. He pulled me back to him and kissed me like he was ready to take me upstairs. At this moment, I wouldn't mind relieving some stress with him, that's for damn sure. I opened the door, and they all yelled welcome home. I saw balloons, streamers, and a banner like it was a birthday party. I said thank you to everyone but then the room got quiet. I turned around and covered my mouth as

I stared at Colby holding a huge pink diamond, while down on his knee.

"Yes. Colby Yes." He stood up and wiped my eyes but didn't put the ring on.

"Journey, the first day I met you, you gave me a run for my money. You were a smart-ass and shy as hell wrapped up in one. The night you came to my party, I saw something in you that told me you would be the one. After that, I was on a mission to make you mine and not from what my pops tried to get me to do but for me. I've been all over and met many women but no one and I mean no one has captivated me the way you have.

I love the way you wake up in the morning and I love watching you sleep. And when you smile I get butterflies in my stomach because I know the woman behind it and she's all mine. Will you marry me Journey Banks?" I had so many tears and snot coming down my face I couldn't speak and just nodded my head. Then, he hugged me tight and we started kissing until Wolf pulled us apart and everyone thought it was funny.

He placed the ring on my finger and had me follow him into one of the rooms.

"But how did you?" I asked and walked over to Armonie's crib.

"Baby, money makes the world go around. Your brothers had a part in this too."

"I love you guys." I gave all three of them a hug and told the nurse I would be back in a few to sit with her. We went back out to where everyone was and ate dinner. Jax and Venus were the first to leave. He didn't want his son staying out too late, and Wolf followed an hour later with his family.

"I'm happy for you Journey. My son and your mom have to be smiling down on the three of you. To see all my grandkids happy is something I didn't think I would live to see."

"Thanks Grams, but I have to get a soundproof room made in this house. How are you going to be telling my brothers Colby be knocking me down?"

"Shit he does. But if you get one, I need one too."

"Don't worry baby. The new house will have all that, and Grams here is getting her own wing. We don't need to hear two cats fighting when she's having sex."

"Oh, no you didn't. Nigga, don't think I don't hear my granddaughter putting work in. You do just as much moaning, and she was a virgin. So she fucking the shit out of you too."

"I'm not denying shit. Journey definitely knows what she's doing in the bedroom. That's why she's about to be my wife. Ain't that right?" I laughed at the two of them. I know I said before that Grams had to go, but I wouldn't be who I am today without her.

"You never cease to amaze me." I told Colby when we were getting ready for bed.

"What?"

"You bought us a house and you're taking my grandmother? You must really love me."

"One, I do love you. I love you very much. Two, I'm having a house built for us. And three, of course I'm bringing her. Grams knows how to cook her ass off, and when you get in your moods, at least I'll still eat."

"You will always eat whether it's food or not?"

"Hell yea, I will. How much longer for you to bleed?" I threw my head back laughing.

"The doctor said I'll probably bleed another week or two, but it's not recommended for me to have sex until my six-week checkup. I can get pregnant fast."

"Who cares if you get pregnant again? You're about to be my wife, and you won't need for anything. You just tell me when you're done bleeding." He told me and laid back in the bed watching TV. I climbed on top of him and kissed his lips, then his neck.

"Stop playing, Journey." I knew I couldn't get any, but I wanted to please my man.

"Mmmm, you don't like the way it feels?"

"You know I do." He said and ran his hands through my hair. I kissed his stomach and above his hairline.

"Don't do it, Journey." He said and sat up. I pushed him back and removed his dick out his boxers. He lifted up a little so I could pull them down."Fuck, Journey. I'm about to cum already." He moaned out, and I continued sucking, slurping, and spitting on him.

"Shit, shit, shit. Awwwww damn baby."

"Mmmmmm, let it all out Colby." I told him and sucked all his cum out. When he was finished, I pulled his boxers back up and laid under his arm.

"That shit right there is exactly why you're going to be my wife."

"I thought it was because you loved me."

"That too, but baby you know just what to do, and I'll be damned if anyone else touches you. I love you."

"I love you too."

"I can't wait to eat that pussy again." He said looking down at me. "You sure you're still bleeding."

"Yes nasty. Go to sleep."

"Hey, I'll be that nasty motherfucker but only for you." He said and pulled the covers up. I think he fell asleep five minutes later.

****

It's been a month since I had Armonie, and she was finally five pounds and able to come out of that damn incubator. When I held her for the first time, it was unreal. She knew my voice and looked around when she heard her father. I told him she was a daddy's girl already. The first time Colby held her, he didn't want to let her go. We took pictures and sent them to everyone. Once they saw us holding her, they all started popping up. I picked Jax up, whose fat ass was almost ten pounds, and he was a month old. Venus said it was because, anytime he cried, Jax would change him and give him a bottle. He didn't want Jax Jr to want for anything. He was very overprotective over Armonie though. He and Wolf both were. If you weren't holding her the way they thought you should, boy were you getting cursed out. I feel bad for my daughter because no one was going to be allowed to date her.

Tonight, Grams and her boyfriend offered to watch the babies while we went out for some drinks. I didn't care to go, but they insisted. Passion was going on six months, and Wolf made her stay home but Darlene came. She was definitely a cool person to hang around with. She didn't take shit from anyone, and you could tell she was madly in love with Drew. I think he was feeling her, too, because the strippers asked him for a dance, and he declined all of them. From what my brothers told me, he loved screwing them so to see that showed me Darlene is doing something right.

"Do you notice the guys acting weird tonight?" I asked Venus, who was staring a hole in Jax while some chick talked to him.

"VENUS?" I yelled out.

"Huh?" I asked her the same question, and she nodded her head yes. We sat in VIP for a while, and I started getting tired. It was after one in the morning, and Armonie would be up at six for a feeding. We were headed out the club, and Colby was hugging me from behind. It felt like there was something hard on his chest, so I turned around to see what it was, then someone had started shooting. People were screaming, running, and trying to hide. I felt him push me to the ground but after the shooting and I got up he was nowhere to be found. I saw people standing over someone shaking their heads but I couldn't get over there in time.

"Let's go, Journey." Wolf said reaching for my hand.

"No. Not until I find Colby." I saw Jax and Venus running to one of the cars.

"Get your ass over here!" He yelled out, and when I stood there, he picked me up and ran with me to his truck. I yelled at him to let me out, but since I was in the back seat, there were child locks on the doors. I picked my phone up and called Colby's phone over and over, and it would ring and go to voicemail. I heard my brother's phone ring, and from the sound of the conversation, it wasn't a good one.

"What happened? Is Colby ok?" He didn't answer and continued driving. He called Jax and told him to meet us at the hospital. I kept asking about Colby, and he kept ignoring me. At the hospital, he opened the door and grabbed me before I was able to run. A few ambulances had pulled up, and I could see them taking a stretcher off. I swore it was Colby, but there's no way it could be him. We were just together. Wolf took me in the waiting room, and we all just sat there not saying anything. No one went to registration or anything.

"Why are we here? We need to go back and find Colby. He's not answering his phone." I yelled out.

"What? Jax you told me they were together." Venus said and started getting upset.

"Fuck this. Is there a Colby Foster here?" I asked the lady at registration. She started typing in his name, and a few seconds later, she gave me a sad face.

"Yes there is someone who was brought in a few minutes ago by that name. Can I ask who you are to him?"

"His wife. Is he ok? Can I go see him?"

"Umm, let me get the doctor to come speak to you." She said and swiped her card to go to the back.

"What is taking her so fucking long?" I yelled out and blew my breath. A few minutes later, she walked out with a doctor. He told us to follow him to a room for privacy. I know when they tell you that, it's bad news. We followed him, and the minute he closed the door, the look on his face told me all I needed to know.

"Mrs. Foster." At first, I thought he was talking to Venus, then I remembered I said I was his wife.

"Just tell me is my husband going to be ok?" My legs were shaking as I waited for him to answer.

"Mrs. Foster, your husband was brought in with multiple gunshot wounds." I covered my mouth and let the tears fall. "Unfortunately, due to where he was hit, by the time he arrived, he had already passed away."

"No. No. No. No. Colby wouldn't leave me. No he wouldn't leave Armonie. You have to go back in there and try to revive him. Please. My husband wouldn't just leave his family like that." I jumped up out my seat.

"I'm sorry ma'am."

"I don't believe you. I want to see him."

"Ma'am, like I stated before. Due to the places he was shot, I'm afraid there's no way you can see him."

"FUCK THAT! How do you know it's my husband then?"

"These are his items that were on his person." He handed me his cell phone, the keys to his car, and his wallet with all his identification in it. I fell to my knees and started screaming. I listened to the voices around me, but I couldn't hear anything. A few minutes later, Wolf picked me up and carried me out to the car. I cried my eyes out in the backseat.

When I got home, my grandmother was at the door with tears in her eyes. I guess she heard what happened. I walked past her and went straight to my daughter's room. I picked her up and took her in the room with me. I could still smell Colby on the sheets and blankets. I don't know when I fell asleep, but when I woke up, it was daytime, and Armonie wasn't in the bed.

I laid there thinking about all the things Colby and I had planned. We were going to have a big wedding and travel with Armonie right after our honeymoon. Then I thought about who wanted Colby dead? I mean, I'm sure he had enemies in his line of work, but to kill him was a coward ass move. There was one person I could think of that I wanted to ask. I hopped out of bed and threw some shoes on. I grabbed the gun Colby left in my nightstand for who knows what, but right now, it came in handy. I didn't wash my face or anything and flew out the door. I started my car and drove straight to the house Colby told me never to step foot in. I only knew where it was, because he had to show me which one it was. I stopped the car, jumped out, and left the door open. I started banging on the door until that bitch of an ex opened it.

"What the fuck you want?"

"Move bitch. Where is that motherfucker?" I bombarded my way in yelling his name.

"FREEDOM?! FREEDOM?! GET YOUR COWARD ASS DOWN HERE." I walked around the downstairs yelling.

"You look like shit." I heard a voice behind me say.

"How could you murder your son?" I pointed the gun at him, and he put his hands up.

"What are you talking about? I didn't murder anyone?"

"You may not have done it, but I bet you had it fixed to be done."

"What is she talking about Freedom?"

"Bitch, don't act like you two don't know Colby was murdered last night." I said and tried to wipe the tears that fell. She covered her mouth, and he had a sad look on his face.

"I didn't know."

"You bastard. I know you had something to do with it." I ran up and started punching him in the chest and face until I dropped to the ground. I felt someone rubbing my back and it was Willow.

"Bitch, don't touch me. You're just as bad as him. I'm sure you know all about his plan. If I were a killer, you two would be dead, but then I'd be no better than you."

"Let's go Journey." I heard my grandmother behind me.

"He killed Colby, Grandma. I don't care what he says." She hugged me and escorted me out the house.

"It's ok baby. He'll get what's coming to him."

"How did you know where I was?"

"When you ran out the house, I followed you. I may be a little old, but I ain't that old." She said, and I got back in my car to follow her home.

******

A week had gone by, and today was the funeral. The entire time, all I did was stay in my room with Armonie. Venus handled the services, and I appreciated her for that. He may have been my fiancé, but that was her brother. My grandmother came in the room and took the baby from me. She told me to get ready, because the limo would be there soon. I don't know what I needed a limo for when I had a car. I threw on my all black Vera Wang wraparound dress, my black red bottoms, and a black hat with the small veil that came down. I didn't want anyone seeing me cry.

When we pulled up to the funeral, it was packed. I didn't even know he knew this many people, but I also knew people were being nosey. Wolf walked Passion in and came back for me, and Jax walked in with Venus. I noticed Wesley sitting on the opposite side next to Willow and his father with a kid on his lap. I had to do a double-take because Colby and Venus never mentioned having a niece or nephew. He nodded his head at me, and I rolled my eyes. I did that because, not once did he stop by or call to check on me. Venus said she hadn't spoken to him either, and that was weird. The three of them used to be tight.

Throughout the service, I kept feeling like I was being watched, but when I turned around, it was nothing. I laid my head on Wolf's shoulder and stared at the casket. It had to be closed due to him being shot in the face. No one told me in detail what he looked like, but I didn't want to imagine it either. After the service and burial was over, I went home. I didn't want to sit at a repast with people saying, "I'm sorry". It wouldn't do anything but make me cry harder. I took my ass straight to bed in hopes that I would wake up and the nightmare would be over.

Colby

Faking my death was probably the hardest thing I had to do besides watching my fiancé almost die. My father made my life a living hell after I went to war with him over Journey, but if I had to do it all again just to be with her, I would. My girl wasn't like any of these women out here; that's why doing this was what was best for both of us. Now that my father was under the impression that I was no longer breathing, he called Wolf and Jax separately and told them he would leave Journey alone, but that now he wanted to pay them to get rid of Wesley. He felt Wesley was my protégé and would eventually end up disobeying him as well.

The night I faked my death, it killed me listening to Journey scream in the other room. I almost ran in there to tell her I was alive, but Drew and my boy Derrick had to hold me back. We had the entire night planned out, and it worked perfectly. I put the vest on when I went in Jax's, office and Drew was the one who did the drive by. The crazy part is he didn't even shoot me. Wolf was able to get Journey out of there fast enough before she noticed, and Derrick came around with the car for me to jump in. I watched Journey and my sister crying at the funeral, and again, I had to hold back. I wanted to tell her but we had to make it look as real as possible.

Tina J.

My girl kept turning around, and I think it was because she felt me watching her. I was up at the top dressed in all black street clothes with my hat hung low and black shades. I put a fake mustache and goatee on to throw people off. I went to make sure my father believed what he saw, and I'm glad he did. Now we had to play the waiting game. I'm not sure if Jax and Wolf would kill Wesley, but after the shit they told me, I didn't care. Who sleeps with their brother's girl and gets her pregnant? I guess, when we broke up she had it, because I damn sure didn't know she was pregnant.

It was two days after my funeral, and Jax and Wolf told me I could go to the house. It was a little after one in the morning when they came and got me from Drew's place. That's where I was staying, and it was cool being that he was never there. He and Passion's sister were getting close and always together.

"You know she's going to curse you out."

"I know, but I'd rather her see I'm ok now than wait months down the line and start messing with someone else." Jax started laughing and gave me the key. At the hospital, they gave her all my stuff, including my keys, so I had no way to get in. I unlocked the door and slid inside. All the lights were off, and there was the night-light glowing in Armonie's room. I went in there, kissed her cheek, and walked out. I didn't want to wake her up just yet. Journey was going to flip, and it would probably scare her.

I opened the bedroom door, and Journey was lying there with her eyes closed. I thought she was asleep, but then I

146

realized she had arched her back and was giving herself pleasure. I saw a few wine bottles on the nightstand. The sight before me had me rock hard. I took my clothes off and slid in between her legs so quick she didn't know what to do. She tried to kick me off and started yelling but I continued to please her.

"Fuck get off me. Who the hell-" She was finally able to back up, and I lost the grip I had on her legs.

"Colby?"

"Yea baby, it's me." She rubbed her eyes to see if she was dreaming.

"Yes, this is a dream. Are you going to allow me to finish pleasing you?"

"Are you sure I'm dreaming?" I told her yes. If I told her no, she would probably be fighting me, and I needed to become one with her again.

"Why did you leave me?" She had her lips pressed against mine and pulled my body on top of hers.

"Just let me taste you." She nodded her head, and I made her cum over and over. I wiped my mouth and slid in between her legs and almost came instantly. I pulled out and played around her entrance for a few minutes and went back in.

"You feel so good, Journey. I miss the hell out of you."

"I missed you too."

"I can't hold out any longer Journey."

"Me either. I'm cumming again."

147

We both stayed in that position for a few minutes. I rolled off of her, and she turned so her back was facing me. I heard her sniffling and turned her to me. I wiped her tears away and held her tight

"Did you do it so you could be with someone else?"

"Hell no. Wait, you're supposed to think I was a dream."

"Do you think I'm that stupid."

"But you were drinking."

"Colby, the second I rubbed my eyes and saw you, I knew it wasn't a dream. I went with it, because I needed to feel you inside me. Now, tell me why you put me through that." She sat up and stared at me. I explained everything to her and she shook her head. "How could you agree to putting me through that?"

"Journey, I didn't have a choice. I would rather him kill me than to take you away." She got up and went to the bathroom. I heard the shower start and got off the bed to get in with her. I grabbed the rag from her and started washing us both up.

"I need to feel you again, Colby." She jumped in my arms and kissed me. I felt myself get hard and slid her down.

"Fuckkkkkk, Journey. God knows I missed my pussy. We continued sexing one another in the shower. When we got out, we had more sex. I think she wanted to make up for our time apart and having our daughter. She put some pajamas on and handed me a pair. After I put them on, she opened the door and told me goodbye.

"Huh?"

"Take your ass in the guest room, and you better pray I forgive your ass."

"I thought you forgave me when you allowed me to make love to you."

"Nope. I wanted you to put another baby in me. That way, when I kill you for that stupid shit you did, at least I'll have two good memories to remind me of you."

"Oh shit. Are you telling me you just used me for my sperm?"

"Yup. And I'm not ashamed to admit it. Now go. You know I go right to sleep after sex." I stood up and walked to the door.

"I love you, Journey."

"I love you, too. Oh, and when I want some dick, I'll come to you. Don't come looking for me." She said and slammed the door. I shook my head and went down the hall to my daughter's room. I lifted her up and checked to see if she needed to be changed and she did. I laid her on my shoulder and went downstairs to get a bottle for her. I missed both of my girls, and if I couldn't sleep with her mom, I was sleeping with Armonie. I turned the kitchen light out, and there stood Grams.

"How did she take it?"

"You want me to keep it one hundred with you?" She gave me a look that told me yes.

"She let me make love to her. Then she fucked the shit out of me and kicked me out the room."

"I taught her well." She said laughing.

"Really, Grams."

"Listen. I know you had to do what you had to, but you have to remember your father tried to kill her and almost succeeded had you not been there. Then, to lose you almost a month later when she was still dealing with that and having a premature baby, she couldn't take it. You should know by now how fragile she is. When my grandsons told me the plan, I wanted to shoot both of them."

"You knew grandma?" Journey said walking in the living room.

"Yes, and I wish you would get an attitude with me. I'm still mad at your ass for trying to be wonder woman and attacking his father."

"YOU DID WHAT?" I yelled and made Armonie jump. Journey put her head down like a kid that just got in trouble by her parents.

"Colby, I thought he killed you, and-"

"And my ass Journey. I made a decision to save your life, and you go over to his house and almost have it taken away. He almost killed you once; you don't think he would've done it again? What if I really were dead? Huh? Who would Armonie have to take care of her? I'm not saying your family wouldn't help, but that was reckless and you better hope I forgive your ass. What I did is nothing compared to what could've happened to you. Grams, take Armonie please. I need to calm down."

I was so fucking mad, yet I couldn't leave the house. I went into the guest room that I put the video game in and turned it on. I had to start a brand new game and use a different name just in case my brother was on and saw my log-in. I was in there for about ten minutes smoking when Journey came in and sat beside me. She turned the ceiling fan on and made sure the door was closed. She tried to talk to me, but I ignored the fuck out of her.

"I'm sorry, Colby. I was mad that he killed you, and I wanted him dead, but I couldn't do it." I blew smoke out and kept playing.

"Colby, please talk to me. You've been away from me for over two weeks, and now that you're back, I want more than ever to talk and lay with you." I saw her wiping her eyes. I swear she cried on demand. She got up to walk out, and I grabbed her hand and pulled her on my lap.

"The only thing that kept me sane being away from you and Armonie was knowing the two of you were safe. If anything had happened to you, I don't know what I would've done. I know you were hurt and wanted to avenge my death, but honey that's not your cup of tea. Journey, don't ever in your life do no dumb shit like that again. Not that we'll be in this situation but anything remotely stupid like that." I moved her lips to mine and parted her mouth with my tongue.

"Take your ass to bed." I smacked her on the ass and had her stand up.

"You're not coming?"

"Ugh, you kicked me out the room." She sucked her teeth and folded her arms. I ignored her and played my game. She didn't move, so I paused my game and looked at her.

"What's up?"

"It's time for bed." I shook my head laughing as she grabbed my hand and tried dragging me off the loveseat we put in there. I put the rest of the blunt out and turned everything off in the room.

"You are so fucking spoiled it's ridiculous." I told her lying down in the bed next to her.

"It's my fiancé's fault." She put her hand out and looked at the ring on her finger.

"I need to talk to him, because it's too much." I told her and we both laughed.

****

The next day, Venus came over and almost had a heart attack when she saw me. She was crying and almost dropped my nephew. If it weren't for Jax, who was standing right there, she might have. He was mad as hell too, and you could see it all over his face. After everyone had calmed down, I broke the news to Venus about my pops and Wesley. She couldn't believe what was going on, or that she had a baby by him.

"Now what? You have to stay inside until they kill dad? I mean, I'm not comfortable knowing that my fiancé is going to kill my father and possibly my other brother?" Venus said wiping her eyes.

"How do you think I feel when I was the one he tried to exterminate first? You think I want them to die? Well, Pops, yea, but not Wesley, but had I not done what I did, who's to say he wouldn't have just come to my house and taken me out? Venus, I know this is hard because once it's done it will only be you and I but it's either us or them. You have to make a decision and you need to talk to your man about the way you're feeling." I told her and went back into the room where everyone else was. Wolf had Armonie lying on his chest and Passion had Baby Jax while Christian played with toys on the floor.

"What's wrong, Venus?" I heard Jax ask her. She told him nothing, but he got up and followed her outside.

"Let me guess. She's mad we have to kill Pops isn't she?" Wolf said.

"Yup, but I told her it's kill or be killed. My dad may not be messing with her, but she can bet he's probably thinking about it.

The rest of the night we ordered food and sat around talking about how we were going to get my dad. Venus got up before the conversation started and went to another room to feed Jax Jr. She didn't want any parts of what was going on. Journey refused to leave, because she didn't want any more fake deaths taking place.

Jax

"What's wrong Venus?" I asked when we finished discussing how we were going to get at her father. She didn't answer me earlier, and I didn't press the issue, but now that we were home, she was going to say something. Her and Jax Jr. were living with me, and this time, I made her give up her house and put it on the market. I wasn't trying to control her, but there was no way my wife would have an extra house somewhere to run off to. We were getting married, and if we argued, then there were plenty of rooms to occupy. She gave him a bath, and I jumped in the shower at the same time. Once my son was asleep, and she had finished getting ready for bed, I pulled her close to me waiting for her to answer.

"Jax, I know you have to do what you have to do, but I just don't know why you have to kill both of them." I blew my breath out, because I knew that was the problem. I just wanted to hear her say it.

"Your dad tried to kill my sister and your brother. Prior to that, he sent your brother to kill both of my parents. Then, he sat inside the Popeye's and told your brother Wesley he had to kill Colby or he would tell his secret. Now that Colby is dead, he wants us to kill Wesley anyway, so you tell me what you think we should do?" I waited for her to answer but she couldn't.

"Exactly. I know it's hard, and I wouldn't do it if I didn't have to, but what if he comes after you or our son next? Your father doesn't care about anyone but himself. If we don't get him first, I can guarantee he will come for us."

"But can't you guys just scare him or something?" I sat up and looked at her like she was crazy.

"Venus, are you just going to skip past the fact that he tried to kill my sister? Matter of fact, he put a hit out on, not one, but both of your brothers. Had we not faked his death, Colby would be dead. He already got your other brother killed. What is it going to take for you to see he needs to be taken care of?" I moved her off my chest and stood up to leave out the room. I loved my girl, but sometimes she acted dumb as fuck, and when she got like that, it was best for me to be away from her.

"Maybe, if I go over there and talk to him." She said on my way out the door.

"No Venus. It's too dangerous."

"Not for me."

"Especially for you. He has you thinking you're not on his hit list but you are."

"Maybe if I take Jax Jr. to meet him." I ran over to where she was and pulled her up by the shirt.

"I'm trying to keep you safe, and all I keep hearing you say is what if you did this or that. I'm done discussing this shit with you. If you want to take your ass over there, then go ahead, but if you think you're about to take my son over there to the man who had my parents killed and tried to take my sister out, you must have lost your fucking mind."

"He's my son, too, and that's my father." She had the nerve to say.

"You're right. He's your father, but that's my motherfucking son. If I even think you're thinking about taking my son over there, I will take him, and you won't ever see him again." I started walking out the room.

"Jax, you can't do that."

"Watch me." I slammed the door, went into my son's room, and wrapped him up in a blanket. I was over this dumb shit she was talking with her dad. I grabbed him some diapers and put that, some wipes, and a few outfits in his diaper bag. I went downstairs, grabbed my keys, and went to Journey's house. I opened the door and found my grandmother sitting in the living room eating ice cream. It was only nine-thirty but it was too late to be eating that.

"She's having a hard time dealing with it huh?"

"Yup, and she thinks taking my son over there will stop him from killing her."

"That child crazy. Don't she know that man don't care about no one but himself?"

"I tried to tell her, but she thinks she knows everything. I love her to death, Grandma, but if she wants to go over there to prove me wrong, then I'm going to let her. At the end of the day, that is her father, but she won't be taking my son with her. That's for sure."

"I hear ya. That is one evil man. Now give me my grandbaby. He's sleeping with Nana tonight." She said and put the ice cream away before taking him in her room. I locked up and went upstairs to one of the guest rooms to lay down. I opened the door and Colby was playing the damn video game.

"What you doing over here?"

"Staying the night. Your sister is bugging, and I had to leave before she made me kill her." He handed me the blunt and a remote control.

"I knew that was going to happen. She can't stand my pops, but she would rather not speak to him, and he know he was alive than to attend his funeral."

"I get that, but it's like she doesn't care that he tried to take you out. I can see my family, but her own brother."

"It be like that sometimes. I'm not mad at all. I have my fiancé, my daughter, and probably a son shortly. I have my family so I'm good."

"You got my sister pregnant again?" I shook my head.

"Most likely. Hey, if it makes you feel better, she told me she used me for my kids." We both busted out laughing, and the door opened. Journey walked in like she had an attitude, and I looked at Colby.

"Don't look at, Colby. Why did you take Jax and leave?"

"Journey, that's not your business." Colby told her, and she gave him the look of death.

"Colby?"

"Don't Colby me. That's not your business. Yes that's your brother, and she's my sister. Stay out of it. If Venus wants Jax, she knows where he is." She turned around and went stomping out the room. I had to bow my head to him. No one, and I mean no one has been able to shut Journey down the way he did. I thought he would run after her, but he picked the remote back up and finished playing the game. He stayed in the room with me for another two hours playing Madden17. Journey came in there two more times asking when he was coming to bed, because she couldn't sleep without him. Venus was the same way with me, and that's probably why she called over here. I shut everything off and went into a different guest room, because the one we were in was too smoky. I used the bathroom and took my ass to sleep.

****

"Fuck, that feels good, Venus. Keep sucking just like that." I moaned out. I didn't have to look to know it was her. She did this thing with her tongue that drove me crazy, and that's exactly what she was doing now. When I was about to cum, she stopped and slid down on top of me.

"Jax, it feels good baby."

"How good?" I asked and smacked her on the ass.

"Good enough to say I'm sorry. Oh gawd, it feels so good. Shittttt. I'm about to cum." She came down harder, and I fucked her from underneath until we both came.

"I'd rather lose him than you. Jax, you and Jax Jr. are my family, and I never want to lose you. I just wanted to-" I kissed her to stop talking.

"It's water under the bridge baby. All that matters is our family. You will still have my sister, brother, your brother, Grams, Passion, Drew, Derrick, and Darlene's crazy ass. Not to mention all the kids. Baby family isn't always blood, remember that." She nodded her head. I lifted her head up.

"Who let your psycho ass in anyway? What if I had another bitch in here?"

"Your sister let me in and you ain't stupid." She said and laid on my chest. We ended up falling asleep in that exact position.

****

I called Wolf up the next day and told him we had to get the situation with Freedom over sooner than later. I know Venus claimed to be on the same page, but it was still written on her face that she doesn't want it to happen. The quicker we get it over with, the faster she can get past it. Colby asked me not to kill Wesley, because that's something he felt he should do, and I could understand. That's like Wolf doing that shit to me with Venus. I wouldn't be able to handle it.

I hung the phone up and walked into the kitchen to make my plate. Grams cooked breakfast for everyone since we were all there. It was crazy looking around the house. She had the drapes closed all through the house just to be sure that, if anyone was watching, they wouldn't see Colby.

The shit last night between him shutting Journey down still had me in awe. That may have happened, but she was still spoiled as hell, and that was going to be a problem. Wolf and I both knew it so he better get ready for it. Venus came in the kitchen with my son and sat next to me. I could see the pain etched on her face, but this had to happen.

"Are you staying over here?"

"Yes. I don't have anything else to do, and Grams said I can't leave without you."

"Why did she say that?"

"Because you told her I was going to take Jax Jr. to see my father, and she said if I did, she was whooping my ass." Colby and I both started laughing. I stood her in between my legs and told her that's what she gets, and that's what was best.

I left the house after giving her and my son a kiss and drove to my house to get some clothes. There was a car sitting in my driveway that I never saw before. I parked behind it and got out when the driver's side door of the other car opened.

"What the fuck you want?" I asked Penny who was coming behind me to the door. "You know I have a girl." I felt her wrap her arms behind me as I put my key in the lock.

"Yea, but she's not here, and I promise if you give me what I want, I won't push the issue with your brother."

"Oh, really." She nodded and stuck her pointer finger in her mouth. I roamed her body and licked my lips. I guess I could take one for the team. Penny was a pretty woman, and I used to be in love with her. There wasn't anything I wouldn't have done for her, but when I got locked up and hit with that bid, she was out. Penny put you in the mindframe of Megan Good but thicker.

"I opened the door and stepped aside so she could enter. She glanced around like she hadn't been here before but she was when she caused Venus to leave when I first came home. I put my phone in my pocket after I sent a message out to Venus.

"Follow me." I said and led her to the office I had downstairs. I would never disrespect my woman by having her in my bed. I closed the door and allowed her to kiss on my neck and feel on my dick.

"Get naked and play with that pussy." I took my shirt off but kept my wife beater on. "Make it nasty for me Penny." She closed her eyes, opened her legs, and massaged her breast while she played with her pussy. It was quite arousing, but that wasn't the point. I sat back in my chair and watched her for a few minutes.

"Make that pussy squirt."

"Are you sure?" She asked but lifted her legs on the chair.

"Do you want this dick?"

"You know I do."

"Then do what I said." I stood up and walked over to where she was and told her to close her eyes and imagine how good I'm going to feel. Venus came in, and I put my fingers up to shush her.

"How does it feel? Are you ready for some of this good dick you missed?"

"Hell yea, Jax. Hurry up, I'm about to cum." She opened her eyes, and I had Venus standing over her with the gun pointed at her forehead.

"What's going on?"

"You're about to die bitch. That's what's going on. You thought my man wasn't going to tell me you came to try and fuck him. Boo, we are one in the same." Venus said and flashed her ring. Women were so extra.

"But Jax, I thought."

"You thought wrong when you tried to set my brother up."

"Then why did you allow me in if you were going to kill me?"

"I had to make sure you weren't wearing a wire. You should've never fucked with my girl or Wolf. Go ahead, Venus." Once I said that, she emptied the entire clip in her.

"That's overkill baby." I told her and took the gun.

"Yea well, I made sure she was dead enough so she can't haunt you in your dreams."

"You know that doesn't make sense right."

"Whatever. I want this entire office remodeled. You won't be reminiscing about any old pussy in here."

"Yea, yea. The only pussy I'm always thinking about is right here." I said and grabbed hers through her leggings.

"It better be or-"

"Or nothing. Don't start talking shit. Your ass will be laid out right next to her." I smacked her on the ass as she walked out. I called the cleaning service to dispose of her and started looking for a company that could remodel that office ASAP.

Wolf

Jax called and explained to me the feelings his fiancé Venus were having but he knew I gave zero fucks about them. She was cool and all, but she may as well get that black dress out now, because Freedom's time was limited. Shit, she better be happy I didn't kill her brothers sooner when I found out who they were. The only reason I didn't kill her pops yet was because I had no idea what he looked like in the beginning or where he resided, but now I have more than enough information on his ass. He should've left the past in the past. I still don't understand why he wants to get at us when his son killed both of my parents, and I supposedly killed two of his sons. Shit, we were even if you asked me.

I pulled into the mall parking lot to pick an outfit up for the baby's christening Journey had planned at her house. She wanted Colby to come so Grams had the party people put tents up in the backyard, and she covered the windows in them. We had to make sure no one came that wasn't invited, because he was supposed to be dead. I hit the alarm on the door and started walking in.

"You're still sexy as hell." I heard behind me. Willow came walking towards me with a sneaky ass grin on her face. Her stomach was poking out, but she couldn't be more than four or five months.

"I sure am." I was a cocky motherfucker, and she wasn't telling me anything I didn't already know.

"Is that dick still big?" I laughed at how pathetic she sounded. Who is pregnant and worried about dick from someone who isn't the father?

"Yup, and my girl enjoys it every night." She bit down on her lip trying to be sexy. I let the electronic mall doors open as she followed behind me trying to make conversation.

"Wolf, let me talk to you real quick." She gestured for me to come with her in the bathroom. The temptation was killing me, but I promised Passion I wouldn't cheat on her, and I wasn't; especially not with a pregnant chick.

"I'm good."

"I guess you don't want to know what Freedom has planned for your family." That piqued my interest being that he said he wouldn't fuck with us like that if we knocked off Colby. I knew he was up to something, because he was too quiet. I guess you can't trust a motherfucker.

"What Willow?" I said standing outside the family bathroom. She opened the door and backed into it grabbing my hand. I looked around, and there were a few different toilets in there, but they each had a separate door. She pulled me in one of them, closed the door behind me and removed her shirt.

"What do you want?" I couldn't even get turned on by her with her stomach poking out like that. Not that I wanted to, but she was too much.

"I want that dick one more time." She got on her knees and tried to unbuckle my pants. She definitely gave good head, but she didn't swallow, and a nigga loved watching Passion do that. I'm not about to fuck up my happy sex life for this. I pulled her up to stand and grabbed her by the hair.

"I'm not playing these games with you bitch. Tell me what the fuck you know now."

"Ok, Wolf, but can you let me go first?" I let go and the bitch started screaming for help. I knew there was a reason I shouldn't have followed her in here. I put my gun under her chin and told her to shut the fuck up.

"You know the type of nigga I am, don't you?" She nodded her head yes and tears started coming down her face. "Why would you assume it was ok to play this game?"

"I don't know Wolf. I'm just doing what he told me."

"What did he tell you?"

"He said to get you in here, because there's no way out. I am supposed to send him a text and let him know when I have you."

"And did you?"

"Not yet. I was going to."

"What is the plan Willow?" I pushed the gun harder under her chin probably leaving an indent.

"Once he kills you off, he's going after Jax and Journey."

"You're just as dumb as your sister was." I backed up and pushed her on the toilet seat.

"What are you talking about?" She asked putting her shirt back on.

"That nigga you pregnant by sent your sister on the same suicide mission you're on right now, and you see what happened to her."

"Please don't tell me you killed her."

"Ok then. I won't." I turned to walk out, and she charged at me and started screaming that I was a murderer.

"Bitch, I'm giving you a chance to walk away, but you're making in hard."

"How could you?"

"Bye Willow." I stood outside the door but still inside the waiting area of the room listening to her. I heard her on the phone telling someone I was in the bathroom. I opened the door she was in and her phone fell out her hand.

"Please don't, I'm pregnant."

"You should've thought about that before you tried to get me killed. You think I give a fuck about that baby?" I let two shots off in between her eyes and sent Jax a message telling him to send the clean-up crew to the mall. I'm not worried about anyone finding her. I locked the door, shut it behind me, and finished shopping. I received a message an hour later saying it was done. I walked out the mall with outfits for me, Passion, and Christian when my phone rang.

"What did you do to her?" I knew that voice from anywhere.

"Freedom? I thought we had an agreement. I see you're not a man of your word; therefore I had to handle some things on my end."

"You couldn't wait until she had my baby?"

"Why should I? You couldn't wait to get at me therefore making things worse. I thought we had a deal." He laughed into the phone.

"That was just to get you and your brother to kill Colby."

"What is your deal? You're going through extreme measures to kill us off." I listened to him fill me in on information that I had been wondering about for the last ten years.

"Your father may have owed me that little bit of chump change I sent Dice to collect, but he had something else that belonged to me too." He said and I could hear him blowing into the phone. He was most likely puffing on one of those nasty ass cigars.

"Oh yea. And what's that?"

"Six million dollars." I chuckled and shook my head.

"Where would my dad get six million dollars from? You say he had it but you saw how we were living." When I turned eighteen that money was given to my siblings and I, but we always wondered what my father did to get it.

"Your father and I were always cool. Actually, we were friends from high school."

"Friends? Yea right. What type of man murders his friend?"

"The type who feels like his friend went behind his back and stole from him."

"Care to explain." I don't even know why I was indulging in the conversation, but I let him finish. I closed the door to my car and pulled out of the parking lot.

"Your father went behind my back and hooked up with a man that was my enemy. The two of them came up with the idea to run their own drug business and that took a lot of customers from me."

"Still doesn't explain where the six million came from."

"He received a loan from me for that amount saying he needed it to get you guys out of the ghetto. I believed him and gave it with no questions asked. Months went by, and it was funny that he had the money, but you were still living in that house receiving government assistance. Long story short, when I found out, I sent Dice there to collect, and he refused to give it up. That little bit of money you assumed he was killed over wasn't it at all."

"Ok, so where's the money you claimed he had?"

"That's still a mystery to me. However, I know he left you with a ton of money in life insurance and stocks and bonds. It would only be right to collect his debt from you." I busted out laughing at him. He must be crazy if he thought for one second I would pay him anything.

"Yea fucking right. This conversation is over."

"Tsk, Tsk, Tsk. Is that any way to speak to the man that will have your sister in my bed soon?"

"Freedom? I'm not going to sit on this phone listening to your threats because that's all they are. You would be a fool to think she's not protected, but I'll continue to allow you to think otherwise."

"The only person that could protect her from me is Colby. You and your brother are busy with our own lives, and well, we all know what happened to him. That leaves her open for me to get at her and that time is coming." He boasted like Colby's death didn't bother him.

"Trust me when I say that's the least of my worries."

"It shouldn't be because its going to happen. That pussy must be good as hell the way she had my son turn his back on his family." He was pissing me off but I wasn't going to give him the satisfaction of knowing it.

"Freedom, I'm going to say this and then our conversation will be over." I heard silence on the phone and checked to make sure he didn't hang up before I spoke.

"I'm coming for you, and when I do, nothing is going to stop me from doing what's meant to be." I said making sure I didn't incriminate myself over the phone. He may have done it quite a few times, but I'm sure he would get around it faster than I would. I hung up and laughed at how stupid he sounded. Colby wasn't going to be happy about him saying that about Journey and would probably want to come out of hiding sooner than later.

I parked in front of my house, and Passion opened the door smiling. I have to admit that she was really changing me and "for the better' as Grams would say. Alternate pussy was good but men get tired of that shit. There's nothing like digging in your woman's pussy knowing you could nut inside without worrying about catching anything. Oh yea, when Passion first moved into the condo the night I brought her home, I told her she had to get to the doctor and get checked out. Her son's father was a hoe and was sleeping around. I don't know why she didn't go sooner, but that was on her. She doesn't know that I saw the negative results on her dresser one day I stopped by when she was at work. That's why I wasn't worried when we had sex. As far as me, I always strapped up and made sure I got checked every six months just in case.

"Hey baby." She kissed my lips and moved out the way for me to come in.

"What up?" I dropped the bags on the floor.

"Nothing. It's late, and Christian is asleep already." She seductively said and pushed me against the door and fell to her knees.

"I love coming home to this." I said and watched her take all of me in.

"And I love giving it to you." She stopped sucking to say. After she pleased me, I made sure to return the favor right there in the foyer. She and I went at it nonstop for over an hour. We both hopped in the shower and went straight to bed afterwards. Sex with us was always good and draining, plus she was the only one I stayed with long enough to get used to me and take every inch. She was definitely going to wear my last name one day.

****

The following day, Passion woke me up to breakfast in bed. I asked her where Christian was since it was early, and she said in his room playing. I watched her come out of the bathroom as I finished eating in just a sheer lingerie set and a satin robe. My man woke up instantly. I moved the tray to the floor, grabbed her hand, and laid her on top of me. I ripped that shit off her and let her slide down.

"Passion, you have some of the best pussy, and you stay wet for me." I moved her body around and pumped harder under her.

"Haven, I need to ask you something." She said and stood on her feet.

"Yea baby." She dropped down, and I smacked her ass making her cream all over me.

"Will you marry me?" She started going faster and squeezing her pussy muscles at the same time. At this moment, she knew I would say yes to anything. I had to gain enough control to stop her because the feeling was too good and I was about to answer her.

"Hold up." I lifted myself up and leaned on my elbows.

"Why did you stop me?"

"What you mean? You don't ask someone a question like that and keep going."

Tina J.

"I'm sorry, Haven. I thought-"

"I know what you thought. You assumed if you fucked the shit out of me, I would automatically say yes. Passion, I love you, don't get me wrong, but you're going about this relationship the wrong way. You asked me to be your man because I took too long to ask you, then you just asked me to marry you, and for what, I don't know." She removed herself off of me when I said that and stood up. I didn't mean to sound harsh, but she had to slow down.

"Just forget it." She walked in the bathroom, and I heard the shower turn on. I sat there shaking my head. Passion and I have been together for a while now, and yes she is the wife and everyone knows it, even though it's not on paper. However, she isn't giving me the chance to ask her anything.

"Passion." I pulled her into my chest when I stepped into the shower behind her.

"It's ok Haven."

"What's ok?"

"You not wanting to marry me." I pushed her back a little to look at me.

"Stop assuming shit and stop trying to ask me first thinking that I'm never going to ask you. That right there will push a nigga away." She nodded her head like she understood but did she?

"Haven?"

"Passion be quiet for a minute and let me talk." I washed her body at the same time I spoke.

"I never thought any woman in this world could come in my life, and do what you did. Matter of fact, I know there isn't one who could. What was supposed to be me looking out for you and Christian ended up with me making the two of you my family? I love the two of you more than I say, and I am working on that. I never want you out there thinking you're not enough or that someone will take your spot, because it's not going to happen." I stood her under the water, let it rinse the soap off, and washed myself up without saying another word. I grabbed her hand and stepped out handing her a towel to wrap herself up.

"Passion, this mushy shit isn't me, and I don't even know what I'm trying to say or if it's coming out right." I grabbed the box off the nightstand and got down on one knee in front of her. I could tell the tears were making her eyes blurry.

"Will you marry me?"

"Yes. Haven. Yes." She jumped in my arms making me fall back. She kissed all over my face.

"Wait, baby." I had to stop her and sit up. I placed the eight-carat diamond on her finger and pulled her body closer for another kiss.

"I love you so much, Haven, and I'm glad you found me that day. I swear, I'm going to make you the happiest man alive." I felt her body moving and was ready to finish what we started, but Christian started crying.

"I promise I got you later, and we can do whatever you want." She winked and threw her robe on to go get him. I knew her nasty ass was talking about anal sex. She and I had discussed it after watching a porno together but never tried it. Yea, we were always looking for new things to spice up our sex life. Sad to say, but Journey put her up on that. I don't want to know what my sister was doing in the bedroom, but whatever it was, that nigga Colby was wrapped around her finger and strung out. I put some boxers and pajama pants on and went downstairs. Passion was feeding him a snack and talking on the phone.

"Calm down, Drew will ask you." I heard her say and knew it was her sister.

"You told your sister already?" I asked shaking my head laughing.

"Baby, I'm excited I'm about to be Mrs. Haven Banks. I had to tell somebody. I know you already told Journey who I'm sure told Venus." She was right; they all knew, but I made sure they didn't tell Darlene, because that bitch talked too much. I don't know how my boy Drew dealt with that, but I did notice that, when she was around him, she wasn't ghetto or loud.

"Just hurry up and get my son ready so we can go." I claimed Christian as my own and was already in the process of adopting him. We may have not been together that long, but he grew on me; my entire family claimed him as well. It was only right. I kissed her cheek and walked out. I didn't feel like hearing her discuss what the ring looked like and whatever else Darlene was about to tell her.

Journey

"Colby, I'm pregnant again." I said riding his dick.

"I know baby." I stopped and looked at him.

"Why you stop? You know I hate when you do that." He pumped under me harder making me regret doing that to him. Colby wasn't a small nigga, and he always fucked my insides up when he made love to me. I didn't mind, but I did try and control the situation that he clearly just took over.

"How did you know? Oh yea, baby. Fuck, I'm cumming." I moaned out and released myself on him.

"The same way any man would know. Your pussy has always been the best, but now that I put my son in there, the feeling is beyond explainable." He flipped me over and lifted my legs over his shoulders then pushed himself in deeper. I tried to speak and couldn't.

"You see how you keep pushing me back when I go deep." He said, and I sucked my teeth. "Yup. You can't take me like you used to but it's all good. It doesn't matter how deep I go; it won't change the fact that you still have the best pussy out there." He let my legs down and stood at the edge of the bed pumping in and out of me. "Fuck me back like I taught you, Journey." He said and I started doing as he asked. "Yea, baby. Got damn, she wet as hell." I loved hearing him talk during sex. It turned both of us on.

"Is this your pussy, Colby?" I asked now stopping him so I could bend over in front of him. He liked when I spread my legs and touched my ankles.

"You know it. Throw that ass back baby." He smacked my ass a few times, and I could feel my pussy squirt. He taught me so much in the bedroom, let alone all the new things we learned watching porn together. Colby knew his way around sex and would encourage me to look at the updated sites to learn new stuff and boy did I. Anal sex was definitely something we tried, and enjoyed, but could do without. The reason was that anal sex was so good that we would get so tired afterwards and not be able to move. It's really hard to explain the feeling but just know it's good. We both agreed that we would do it at least once a month unless the other wanted it before then which sometimes happened.

"Spread those cheeks for me." I knew he was about to cum. I could feel his body stiffening and his moaning got a little louder. I moved forward, turned around to get on my knees, and sucked until all his cum was out. He pulled me up and grabbed my ass.

"Fuck girl. You have never done that before, but thank you." He said sticking his tongue in my mouth.

"You know how to thank me." I told him and laid back on the bed with my legs opened.

"You damn right I do. I'm hungry, too. Bring that pussy to me since you didn't let me taste it yet." He climbed on the bed, and just as he was about to indulge, my grandmother came knocking on the door.

"Ok, you two motherfucking perverts. People are starting to pull up, and don't nobody want to hear you in here moaning. Journey, hop off the dick, and Colby, pull out the pussy. Chop. Chop. It's party time." She said making us both laugh.

"Fuck that. I need a snack." He said and gave me two back-to-back orgasms. He lifted himself and wiped his mouth with the back of his hand. I could taste my juices on his tongue as he kissed me.

"Come on baby. It's almost time." I told him, and we took a shower together to save time. We wore all white with him wearing the new all white Jordan's that just came out. I went to Armonie's room and dressed her in the christening dress with her ballet-like shoes to match. I brushed her hair down and put the white headband around it. Grams escorted the picture guy up so we could take pictures before the service. Twenty minutes later, my brothers came in the room, and we had the kids who were all dressed in white take photos together and then they took their own family pictures. It was a good hour and a half before we were done. I walked downstairs, and no one was even here yet.

"Grams, I thought you said people were here."

"That was the only way I could keep you two from being loud. I see it didn't stop you though. Your ass was still up there calling for God when I left." I covered my mouth and Colby grabbed me by the waist.

"A few more weeks and the house will be done. She won't hear either one of us moaning. You can be as loud as you want." He kissed my neck and took Armonie from me. Not too long after, Wolf and Jax stayed in the living room monitoring the guests who were coming. After everyone we invited was there, which weren't many, they locked the front door. It was mainly my brothers' friends and their women with kids, a few chicks from the beauty salon and some of the people I went to school with. No one was allowed to take pictures and had to sign a confidentiality agreement. We couldn't let it out that Colby was alive.

The reverend started, and throughout the christening, Armonie was good until Colby handed her to him, and he started sprinkling water on her. She was screaming her head off. When he finished with Armonie, Jax Jr went through the same thing and my brother thought it was funny. Venus smacked him on the arm and told him he wasn't getting any later if he didn't stop. Yes, she said it loud enough for everyone to hear.

After both of the kids were finished, the DJ started playing music, the party started, and everyone seemed to be having a good time. The men were drinking and smoking, so I took my daughter upstairs. A few minutes later, Venus brought Baby Jax in and little Christian came in with Passion. All of them were knocked out. We laid them down and went back outside.

"What you doing here?" I heard Venus say when she opened the door. I looked, and it was Wesley.

"Passion, go tell Wolf that he has to hide Colby. Wesley is here, and I know he'll tell their father." I whispered to her. She walked fast outside, and I could see out the corner of my eye that Colby was coming in and going into the kitchen. I didn't see him come out and went to see what was going on.

"Hey, Journey." I heard Wesley say and turned around to see him standing there licking his lips.

"Hi, Wesley. What are you doing here?" He moved closer to where I was and handed me a card. I damn sure wasn't opening that. I learned my lesson from the flowers and didn't want a repeat.

"Why wouldn't I be? My niece is getting christened today. I wouldn't miss that." I wasn't sure how he found out, because no one spoke to him as far as I knew.

"Oh, well you missed it." I said and walked out the door to where everyone else was. He made me very uncomfortable, and I would be a fool to stay in there with him alone. He spoke to everyone, but you could tell no one cared for him by the way he received the dry hellos. I think he knew too.

"Can I talk to you real quick?" I heard Wesley behind me when I walked in the kitchen to bring out some more food. I turned around, and he had me backed up against the wall. I looked outside, and everyone seemed to be engaged in their own world.

"What Wesley?" I pushed him and walked towards the front door. He followed and grabbed me. He started smelling my neck and pushed me back up against the wall again.

"I see you're fucking someone else now that my brother is no longer among the living." I laughed because he had no idea.

"I guess you weren't loving him that much if you have these hickeys on your neck."

"Wesley, what I do is none of your business."

"It is my business when I want some too."

"What? Wesley, Colby was your brother."

"Exactly. Was?" His hand roamed my body, and I was disgusted.

"Wesley, it's time for you to go."

"Not before I taste what had my brother going crazy." He said and covered my mouth with his hand and forcing me into one of the rooms. I tried to run out, but I heard a gun cock and that stopped me in my tracks.

"You're going to give me some of that pussy before I end your life." I felt the tears running down my eyes. No one knew where I was, and this nigga was about to rape then kill me. If I screamed, he would kill me so I just stood there. He swung my body to him and lifted my dress up.

"That pussy is beautiful Journey. I see why my brother was going crazy and I haven't even tasted it yet."

"You're going to rape your brother's wife?"

"You're a widow, and I'm going to take it the same way I did with Willow. The only difference was the bitch kept the baby." I covered my mouth in shock. Colby told me they had a baby together, but I didn't know it was because he raped her. I thought he just didn't like her because she was a bitch.

"Wesley, please don't do this."

"I have to. You see, from the moment I saw you that day at my brother's house, I wanted you in the worst way. The way you made him chase you and then how quick you had him fall in love made me want you even more. I knew my father wanted him dead, because we discussed me being the one to do it. Unfortunately, someone got to him before I did. Now that he's not here, it's only right that you share what made him lose his life."

"What are you talking about?" I asked, trying to distract him, and it was working for the moment. I prayed someone came looking for me soon.

"If he would've killed you like he was supposed to, he would still be here right now. Oh, but then you would be dead. Now that's enough talking bitch. You think I don't know you're trying to distract me? Too bad it's not working because the sight of your pussy is calling me." I saw how hard he was. He pushed me back on the bed and climbed on top of me. I was yelling for him to get off me but he wouldn't and he was too heavy for me to move.

"Get the fuck off my wife." Wesley's entire body froze when he heard that gun cock and Colby's voice. He didn't

move fast enough so Colby hit him in the head with the butt
of the gun. Blood started shooting out everywhere. He rolled
him off me and pulled me up.

"You ok baby?" He moved my hair out my face and kissed
my tears. "Stop crying, Journey. What are you doing in here
with him?"

"Baby, I was in the kitchen and… and he, he grabbed me
and-" I couldn't get the story out because I was crying so
much.

"It's ok. I'm going to handle it. Go out there and clean
yourself up. Tell your brothers to call the clean-up crew and
be ready to ride out when I'm done. This shit ends now." He
kissed me aggressively and shoved me out the door.

"Oh my God, Journey, are you ok?" Venus came running
to me the minute he pushed me out the door. I looked down,
and that's when I realized I had specks of blood on my white
outfit. I ran upstairs with her, Passion, and Darlene right
behind me. I picked my cell up and sent a message to Jax and
Wolf who came barging into my room just as I was about to
step in the shower.

"What the fuck happened and where is Colby?" I heard
Wolf yell out.

"Hold on. I have to get this blood off me." I said and
closed the door. I figured the guys would be gone when I got
out, but they were sitting right there. Thank goodness I
brought my clothes in there with me. I told them what

happened, and both of my brothers' eyes looked as if they turned a different color.

Venus and Passion both looked at me. and I shrugged my shoulders. I was seeing the same thing they were. but I was used to it. You had to get them really, really mad to see that. The other time it happened was when my parents were murdered and they found out Colby pulled a gun out on me. They both ran out the room and so did the rest of us. I watched Colby come out the room and ask them where I was. He came straight to me and wrapped his arms around me.

"I love you, Journey, and I swear it's almost over."

"I love you' too. Be careful."

Wolf told everyone the party was over. and Jax made sure everyone left. The girls and I cleaned up and were told to lock up and stay in Grams' room with the kids. That way, if anyone came, she had a gun, and we were all together. My man kissed me on his way out like my brothers did their fiancé's. I said a silent prayer that my man would make it back safely.

Colby

I saw Passion when she went running over to Wolf to tell him something, and I was talking to Grams about surprising Journey after the party to tell her the house was ready and that we could move in any time. I saw Wolf walking towards me and thought something was wrong with Journey or my daughter. When he told me my brother was there, I was pissed because that meant my pops sent him, but how did they find out about it? I slipped in through the back door and saw Wesley handing her a card. She threw it on the counter, and that made me happy, because anything could be in the card. Wolf had me go in some room and wait until he came back to get me. I sat in there pacing back and forth for what seemed like hours. It felt like they were taking too long so I looked out the window to see if Journey was back outside; when she wasn't I said fuck Wesley and went looking for her.

I opened the door and went to the kitchen and she was no longer in there. I opened the card that was still on the counter, and it had two hundred dollars in it.

Dear Armonie, sorry that you only met your mommy for a short time. Don't worry; she'll be in hell alongside your father.

I read what he wrote and ran through the house looking for her. I opened up a few doors and nothing. The last door I opened, he was on top of her trying to kiss her, and I could hear her telling him to get up. I was mad as hell at him, but more pissed at myself for not watching over her better. I shut the door after she left and sat on the bed staring at him lying on the floor with his head bleeding.

"Why Wesley?" I asked as he tried wiping the blood that was coming down his face from where I hit him.

"Why what?"

"Why are you trying to rape my woman? Why are you even here?"

"Man, ain't nobody try to rape her, and how are you alive?"

"NIGGA, I WALKED IN WITH YOU ON TOP OF HER! SHE WAS TELLING YOU TO GET UP! WHAT YOU THINK GET UP MEANS?"

"Please. She wanted it just like Willow did." And then I remembered about the two of them. I could care less at this point that he fucked her, but at the time, I was in love with Willow.

"Wait a minute. Did you rape Willow?" I asked waiting for him to answer.

"It's not rape if she allowed me to do it more than once." I stood up with my gun still in my hand shaking my head.

"All this time, I thought you hated her because she cheated on me. I thought you had my back, and the entire time you were doing that. What about your son? Are you going to teach him that same shit? What am I asking you that for? You're not leaving this room alive."

190

"Colby, I'm only doing what I saw pops doing to mom all these years. Yes, I was a product of his outside marriage. After I was old enough to, he would come by and I would hear my mom and him in the room arguing. He would tell her to strip and she would tell him no. The next thing I know, you could hear the headboard banging against the wall. My mom was screaming for him to get up, but she didn't make him."

"You fucking idiot. I've seen your mom, and she is tiny. How did you expect her to get our big ass father off of her? I can't believe this shit."

"Colby, I'm sorry man. Dad got in my head and-"

"Shut the fuck up. Wesley, you were my brother. MY FUCKING BROTHER, MAN! So what if we had different moms; you were still my blood. You should've come to me, and we could've gotten you some help. Never mind that; why would you go after Journey? You know she means everything to me."

"I don't know. She changed you and made you a different person. I'm not going to lie; she is everything I want in a woman. You were gone; and I was told I had to kill her; but I wanted to sample her first." The second he said that, I shot him straight between the eyes. To even think about another man, let alone my brother, thinking about my woman's pussy had me seeing red. I let off a few more shots and walked out the room. The first people I ran into were her brothers. I looked up, and she was running down the steps to me.

"I love you, Journey, but this shit ends now." I lifted her chin and kissed her.

"I love you, too. Colby, please be careful." I wiped her tears and hugged her. I listened to the guys tell the girls to stay in one room after everyone was gone. I gave her one last look on my way out the door and mouthed the words I love you to her. It was time for me to finally take my pops out.

"You good?" Jax asked as we all sat there putting bulletproof vests on. My dad was no longer staying in his house anymore and had security so tight you would think he was the president. However, my aunt that was staying with me, his sister, gave me all the information I needed to get in. She hated him for trying to kill me and doing the same with Wesley. She was the one that helped him raise Venus and I when my mom passed, and now she had to take care of my brother's kid.

"Hey aunty, we good over there." She didn't like for me to call her by her name for some reason. I think she liked aunty because it made her feel young.

"Yup. He just got here and went straight to his room. Paco is waiting for you at the service entrance. Remember there is a guard at the end of every hallway, but none of them have more than one gun. However, the two guarding your father's room both have vests and machine guns so be careful.

"Ok, thanks aunty."

"You're welcome, nephew. I love you." She said and hung the phone up. We took the thirty-minute drive to his estate

192

that was hidden back in the woods. If we didn't want to be seen, we had to park our cars on the road and walk. There were five carloads of us and nothing but land. She told me where the cameras were and how to get around them. There may have been a lot of us, but we moved like ghosts through there. We got to the service door, and I knocked once and then thirty seconds later knocked again. That was the code to get in. Paco and I were not acquainted with each other so we had to come up with a way for him to know who I was. He shook our hands when we stepped in and closed the door behind us. There was about ten of us inside the house while the rest surrounded the outside.

"Ok. Let me fill you in real quick," Paco said. He told us there were a total of thirty guards in the house, and that included the two at my pops' bedroom door. There was also a butler and maid that were ride or die for him as well and not to take them at face value. Finally, he told me there would be a surprise when we got into my pops' room. Jax and Wolf looked at me, and at the moment, I could care less. I just wanted him dead, and the sooner, the better.

We each split up and ran through the house dropping body after body. I ran into the maid who couldn't be any older than thirty and her uniform was way too short. I'm sure she was probably sleeping with my father. I watched her lick her lips as she stared me up and down.

"Who are you?" She came closer, and I stopped her in mid-stride.

"You think you're slick. Let me see what's under that dress." She tried to do it slowly. Jax and Wolf both walked up as she did it.

PHEW! PHEW! PHEW! PHEW! Gunshots were going off throughout the house, and the maid stood there smirking.

"I don't know why you're smirking because you're about to die." She wiped that shit right off her face, and the bullet went straight through her skull. We got to the third floor where my dad's room was, and the two guards were laughing and had their ear to the door. What type of security does this shit?" We didn't have to worry about shit because them not paying attention caused them to lose their lives. Their bodies dropped in front of the door. Wolf and I kicked the door open and got the surprise of our life.

"Journey, Venus what the fuck are you doing here?" I yelled out but couldn't keep my eyes off Journey. She had on a pair of black tight ass spandex pants with a tight shirt to match. Her body was just right in that outfit, and I felt myself adjusting my dick. Venus had the same thing on, and Jax was in the same trance that I was.

"Are you two strung out motherfuckers serious right now?" Wolf yelled out.

"Hey baby." Journey said and walked to me. I yanked her by the hair and put my tongue in her mouth. If it weren't for where we were, I would've fucked the shit out of her.

"Shit, Journey. You look good as hell in this."

"I know right. Your aunt picked it out for us, and when we put it on, I took a few pictures for you. You know I'm going to handle that when we get home right?" She whispered in my ear and stuck her tongue inside.

"Yo, Journey back up. I don't give a fuck that you're about to get married." Jax said, yanking her up but not hard.

"Ok. Ok." She pecked my lips and went back to where my pops was. They had him tied up naked with just boxers to a chair. There was duct tape on his mouth, and it looked like they were beating the hell out of him with a belt.

"How did this happen? I mean, who let y'all in here."

"I did." Grams came out the bathroom fixing her clothes. This entire time I forgot that she wasn't in the house when we left. I thought she helped the girls clean up but I guess not.

"When y'all were cleaning the house, I was already on the road coming here. Your aunt and I have been talking every day about setting this motherfucker up. I'm the one that told your father about the christening, because I knew he would send Wesley. The moment he walked in, I told Wolf and Jax not to kill him because that was your kill."

"Thank you."

"Anyway, to make a long story short, so he can go to hell where he belongs, I had your aunt give me his number and got reacquainted with him if you know what I mean."

"Yuk, Grams." Jax said making us all laugh.

"What about your boyfriend?" I asked her, and she told me what he don't know won't hurt him. She loved him and would never cheat on him, but in order to protect her family, she had to do what she had to do. I could respect that, but I wished Journey would.

"And how did you two beat us here?" Jax asked Venus.

"Aunty was in the car waiting for us when you left. We knew you guys were going to make a few pit stops to round everyone up." She answered and gave him a peck on the lips.

"Today was a setup minus the part with what your brother tried to do with my granddaughter, but this was happening tonight regardless."

"How did they get in the room?"

"Do you see how they're dressed? The guards took one look at them and assumed it was an orgy and let them right in. They don't know who Venus is since your dad never spoke of her or had no photos of her in the house. Your father was getting out the shower as they walked in. By the time he realized what was going on, it was too late. Venus had already hit him over the head with her gun."

"I taught you well baby." Jax pulled her in and kissed her.

"Colby, I know this is your father, and you want to take his life, but honestly, I think my grandkids are owed that, don't you think?" I looked at Venus, who nodded her head yes, and my aunt did the same when I looked at her. I didn't even realize she slipped in the room.

"Journey, you've never take a life. Are you sure this is what you want?" I asked her after Grams said that. My father was squirming in his seat, and for the first time ever, I saw fear and regret in his eyes, but I had no clue who it was for, nor did I care.

"Colby, I love you for loving me the way you do, but this is something I have to do. I know he isn't the one who pulled the trigger, and I wish your brother was alive so I could kill him, but this is as close as I'll get to avenging my parents' death."

"I'm not trying to tell you what to do, but I don't think it's a good idea. I mean, one of your brothers can do it. Baby, they're used to it, and I don't want you to have nightmares."

"Colby, it's ok. If I do have nightmares, I know you'll be right there to comfort me. Please let me do this." I could see the pain in her eyes as if she didn't get this moment it would hurt her.

"Colby just let her do it. She needs to get past it, and if this is the only way, then so be it." Venus said, and I looked at her brothers. Both of them nodded their head yes and Grams told me to hurry up because she was tired of listening to him make noises. I handed her my gun.

"Thank you, Colby." She said and kissed my lips. She grabbed Jax and Wolf's hands and stood in front of my father. Wolf hit him so hard he was out for a few minutes. When he opened his eyes Jax started beating on him until he got tired. Grams stood on the side watching with the rest of us. As my father sat there barely breathing my fiancé said some shit that had us all at a loss for words.

"Freedom, my brothers and I are standing in front of you to make sure we are the last people you see before I take your life. I don't want you to beg for your life nor do I want you to feel bad for yourself. You destroyed our family all those years ago and tried to do it again using your own son. However, you messed up, because God put him in my life for a reason, and that reason brings us all here today. My parents didn't deserve to die, no matter what the situation, but you took their life anyway. As far as those millions you say he had, you lied and told my brother is was over drugs, when in all actuality that was the money my dad inherited from his own father." I looked at Grams, and she nodded her head yes.

"See, I did the research when Wolf told me what you said, and my grandfather was a gambler. One day he went down to Atlantic City and won six hundred thousand dollars. He invested that money in drugs and ended up with six million dollars. You were just coming into the game because you dealt more in the gun trade, and my father confided in you about that money, and instead of you being happy about it, you tried to take it like the greedy bastard you are. Since he didn't give it to you, you sent your oldest son on a wild goose chase and got him killed for money that didn't belong to you." I looked over, and Venus and my aunt were crying their eyes out. None of us knew my father was shady like this.

"I want to say that you may have taken our parents, but in return, God took two of your sons and that baby that Willow had in her stomach that you were upset about. You cared more about revenge than anything, and that much hatred put you where you are today."

I saw her lift the gun and place it on his forehead. My pops was crying and you could see that he used the bathroom on himself. Who knew he was scared to die? You wouldn't know by all the lives he took.

"Have fun in hell motherfucker." She said and emptied the entire clip in his head. Blood was all over her face as well as her brothers. Nobody said a word as the three of them stood there hugging. This was a moment that they needed, and even though I lost my father, I gained three brothers because they claimed Drew as their brother too, and a grandmother who didn't take any shit. Drew came walking into the room eating a sandwich.

"What are you doing eating at a time like this?" Grams asked when she saw him.

"I don't know, Grams. I've been eating like crazy lately. I think I need to go to the doctors or something."

"No stupid. You done got that girl pregnant, and you probably got her symptoms."

"Oh, hell no."

"Don't hell no now. You need to bring her ghetto ass back to the house so I can have my talk with her." Drew didn't say shit.

"I love you baby." Journey said and jumped into my arms crying. I walked out with her in the same position and stood her up outside the room.

"I'm proud of you baby. I know it took a lot out of you."

"It did, but I feel free now. Are you mad at me?" She asked, and I took my shirt off to wipe the blood off her face.

"Why would I be mad?"

"Because I killed your dad."

"I could never be mad at you for that. If I had known all that had happened, I would've brought you here to kill him when we first met." I continued wiping her face and neck while she stared at me. She still held the same innocence that she had when we first met. She may have committed her first and only murder because there was no way I would allow her to do that again, but she was still pure and innocent in my eyes.

"Let's get you home and cleaned up."

"Aunty, I need you to order her another one of these outfits. This one has blood on it, and let's just say, you know what' never mind. Can you order her another one?" I asked, and she started laughing but told me yes. I went home that night and made love to her until she begged me to stop. I held her tight and said a prayer to God thanking him for sending her to me. She was definitely the woman of my dreams.

Jax

I was shocked by the way Venus handled the situation with her father. She had a hard time dealing with me taking him out, but I guess since it was Journey it was different. My sister was no killer, but I think she handled the situation perfectly. When she told everything their father did, I saw Venus crying, and I wanted to console her, but she had to wait. This moment was ours, and we waited a long time for it.

When Journey pulled the trigger, it was like the weight was lifted off of us. My parents being killed took a lot out of all of us. I was ok once Wolf took out the brother, but this entire time, she thought no one was held responsible for their deaths, and we kept it that way up until he tried to kill Wolf. We were always tight, and even though she didn't see me in jail, we wrote each other twice a week and talked on the phone almost every day. I may have been absent in sight, but mentally and emotionally, I was there for her and my brother.

"You ok, Venus?" I asked her when we got home from her father's. After Colby took Journey home, everyone else started following suit. Their aunt packed up and left to stay with us until Colby moved my sister to their new place in a few days. She told his aunt that she was more than welcomed to stay there with the kids. It was more than enough room, and the kids would love the pool; the school system was good too. She and Grams hit it off well and were already talking about going out with us this weekend to celebrate Wolf and Passion getting married. He proposed this morning, but with everything going on, he couldn't even enjoy the moment.

"I'm good, baby. I thought I would be mad that his life was taken, but hearing everything he did put a lot of things in perspective for me. Thank you for being here for me baby. I love you."

"I love you, too, and I'm going to always be here. You know that." She and I had sex all night off and on. I'm sure she was pregnant by the number of times I let off in her.

****

The next night, we met everyone at the club and partied like none of us had kids at home. Grams had her boyfriend there, and Venus' aunt had the dude Paco there. Evidently, they had been shacking up for a while.

"Let's make a toast." I heard Journey say.

"That better be soda in that glass." Colby said taking it from her and sipping on it.

"Of course it is." She smiled, and just like that, his attitude was gone. I can admit that I wasn't feeling the two of them together, but the way they complimented each other and had each other's back reminded me of my parents. I was happy that we all found the perfect match. Passion lifted her glass up and spoke first.

"I want to make a toast to my fiancé, Wolf. A man who I fell in love with and who has accepted my son as his own with no questions asked. I love you, Haven Banks." She stood in front of him and planted a wet kiss on him.

"I want to make a toast to my fiancé Jax, who loved me enough to put me in my place about my father. I love how you take care of our son, and how you protect us at all costs. I love you." She kissed me, sat on my lap, and grinded on my dick trying to be funny. I popped her ass and told her to cut it out or we were going to my office. She told me after we all made a toast that's what she wanted anyway.

"To my fiancé, my lover, my best friend, and my protector, Colby. I love you with everything I have, and I love the way you love me. You aren't afraid to express the way you feel to me nor are you afraid of my brothers. You went to war with them to be with me, and I love you even more for that. You are anything I could ever ask for in a man, and I'm glad you chose me to be the woman you spend the rest of your life with. I love you baby." Of course, they had to be extra nasty with their kiss until Wolf pulled Journey back. We know they're about to be married, but we still didn't want to see that.

"Last but not least, to the SAVAGES." Wolf yelled out, and we all stood up.

"To the SAVAGES." Everybody said and took a sip of their drink. We were sitting there talking when we heard Jay-

Z's song "Ain't no nigga". We all sung along with the chorus, but the girls were singing something different.

"Venus, what are yall saying?" I pulled her away to ask.

"Do you hear when he says ain't no nigga?" I nodded my head yes.

"Well, we are singing Ain't No Savage Like The One We Got." I just shook my head laughing. These girls were a trip, but I wouldn't change a thing on how we all ended up.

The End

CPSIA information can be obtained
at www.ICGtesting.com
Printed in the USA
LVOW13s1431150218
566731LV00022B/596/P